KEEPERS

OF THE

LOST ARK

A James Acton Thriller

Also by J. Robert Kennedy

James Acton Thrillers

The Protocol	*Pompeii's Ghosts*	*Wages of Sin*
Brass Monkey	*Amazon Burning*	*Wrath of the Gods*
Broken Dove	*The Riddle*	*The Templar's Revenge*
The Templar's Relic	*Blood Relics*	*The Nazi's Engineer*
Flags of Sin	*Sins of the Titanic*	*Atlantis Lost*
The Arab Fall	*Saint Peter's Soldiers*	*The Cylon Curse*
The Circle of Eight	*The Thirteenth Legion*	*The Viking Deception*
The Venice Code	*Raging Sun*	*Keepers of the Lost Ark*

Special Agent Dylan Kane Thrillers

Rogue Operator	*Black Widow*
Containment Failure	*The Agenda*
Cold Warriors	*Retribution*
Death to America	*State Sanctioned*

Delta Force Unleashed Thrillers

Payback	*The Lazarus Moment*
Infidels	*Kill Chain*
	Forgotten

Templar Detective Thrillers

The Templar Detective
The Templar Detective and the Parisian Adulteress
The Templar Detective and the Sergeant's Secret
The Templar Detective and the Unholy Exorcist

Detective Shakespeare Mysteries

Depraved Difference
Tick Tock
The Redeemer

Zander Varga, Vampire Detective

The Turned

KEEPERS OF THE LOST ARK

A James Acton Thriller

J. ROBERT KENNEDY

ISBN: 9781998005420

First Edition

10 9 8 7 6 5 4 3 2 1

For Glen Goudie, taken from us far too soon.

You will be missed, my friend.

KEEPERS OF THE LOST ARK

A James Acton Thriller

"And it shall come to pass, when ye be multiplied and increased in the land, in those days, saith the LORD, they shall say no more, The ark of the covenant of the LORD: neither shall it come to mind: neither shall they remember it; neither shall they visit it; neither shall that be done any more. At that time they shall call Jerusalem the throne of the LORD; and all the nations shall be gathered unto it, to the name of the LORD, to Jerusalem: neither shall they walk any more after the imagination of their evil heart."

Jeremiah 3:16-17, King James Version

PREFACE

Our art, whether paintings by the masters, or movies made by Hollywood moguls like Steven Spielberg and George Lucas, have given us a consistent image of how the Ark of the Covenant should appear. What many don't know, is that their inspiration has always been the extremely detailed description provided in the Bible. Exodus describes it in detail:

"They shall construct an ark of acacia wood two and a half cubits long, and one and a half cubits wide, and one and a half cubits high. You shall overlay it with pure gold, inside and out you shall overlay it, and you shall make a gold molding around it. You shall cast four gold rings for it and fasten them on its four feet, and two rings shall be on one side of it and two rings on the other side of it. You shall make poles of acacia wood and overlay them with gold. You shall put the poles into the rings on the sides of the ark, to carry the ark with them. The poles shall remain in the rings of the ark; they shall not be removed from it. You shall put into the ark the testimony

which I shall give you. You shall make a mercy seat of pure gold, two and a half cubits long and one and a half cubits wide. You shall make two cherubim of gold, make them of hammered work at the two ends of the mercy seat. Make one cherub at one end and one cherub at the other end; you shall make the cherubim of one piece with the mercy seat at its two ends. The cherubim shall have their wings spread upward, covering the mercy seat with their wings and facing one another; the faces of the cherubim are to be turned toward the mercy seat. You shall put the mercy seat on top of the ark, and in the ark you shall put the testimony which I will give to you. There I will meet with you; and from above the mercy seat, from between the two cherubim which are upon the ark of the testimony, I will speak to you about all that I will give you in commandment for the sons of Israel."

Those who believe, will not doubt that the Israelites followed their instructions to the letter, as did generations of artists.

What many, if not most, have overlooked, is the prophecy delivered by the Lord in Jeremiah 3:16-17, in which He tells of a time when the Ark will have been forgotten, there no need to remember it, as all man will be united under Him in Jerusalem.

And what better way to forget something that has been lost, than to destroy it before it can ever be rediscovered?

Ethiopia

Present Day

"I'm on my last mag!"

Archaeology Professor James Acton nodded, picking a target and squeezing the trigger, one of the many rushing their position grabbing for his stomach before crumbling to the ground. He glanced over his shoulder at his wife, Professor Laura Palmer. "Me too! Make them count!"

"There are too many of them! They're not giving me any time to line up a shot!"

Acton fired another precious bullet, eliminating another of their too close enemy before ducking, a hail of gunfire nearly finding its mark. "Let them get closer!"

"Closer? Are you barmy?"

"Obviously, I married you!"

Laura laughed then popped up, taking a single shot before dropping back down. He heard the grunt of someone rushing their position and rose, firing and catching the man in the shoulder, but not before someone returned the favor. He cried out and collapsed, grabbing at his shoulder, the pain quickly subsiding.

"Are you okay?"

"Yeah, just a graze. Left shoulder. I'll live."

"Too bad. It would have meant I could use that bullet you were saving for yourself."

He laughed, amazed at how calm she was knowing what was about to happen. "God, I love you so much!"

Their enemy seemed to sense they had won, and sustained gunfire rained on their position, tearing apart the ground above them as they huddled in the stairs carved into the ancient stone.

"I think this is it," he said, taking Laura by the shoulders. "I love you!"

"I love you too!"

"See you on the other side?"

She nodded, tears in her eyes, his own burning. He grabbed her, hugging her hard for the last time, then jumped up, firing what remained of his bullets on full auto, and cursing the day he had ever met the Keeper of the Ark.

Royal Palace of King Solomon

Jerusalem, Kingdom of Israel

10th Century BC

It wasn't that he was handsome, it was that he was powerful. She had never met such a man before, though she had met kings before. Yet none were like this one. King Solomon, leader of the Israelites, was powerful, wealthy, confident, intelligent. He was everything any woman would want.

If they wanted to be kept.

She was a queen, and though her people were not as mighty as the Israelites, they were equally as proud, as she was to lead them. And the Queen of Sheba would be second to no one.

No matter how obsessed her host was with her.

She was a novelty in his court. A dark-skinned woman from a land the wise King Solomon knew little about. She had proven her wealth with the generous gifts she had brought, demonstrating her kingdom was mighty.

And King Solomon had been generous as well. Not only with his daily gifts to her, but his hospitality, and willingness to share his wisdom. And that was why she had come. An emissary she had sent to the Israelites had returned with stories of Solomon, and she had become determined to meet him. Her journey had been long and difficult, though now that it was coming to an end, she had no regrets, the time away from her people well worth it.

She looked forward to seeing her kingdom again, despite Solomon's repeated pleas for her to stay. It was obvious he was infatuated, and he had even proposed marriage. Though to be one of his hundreds of wives was of little interest to her, despite his insistence she would be first among them all.

She loved her people, and would take a husband when she returned, ensuring her royal line would continue, though under her own control.

She took a drink of wine, the food tonight particularly flavorful, if not a little too salty, and spicy, for her liking. She noticed her host, staring at her once again. "Is there something on your mind?"

He smiled as he took a generous draw of his own drink. "You, of course, Makeda."

Makeda wagged a finger. "You know what I said. I must return to my people a free woman. And besides, you know as well as I do that your interest in me is merely because I am different than any queen you have seen before."

He smiled. "While it is true that others' beauty pale in comparison to yours, it is your mind that enthralls me. Our conversations are the most riveting that I can recall, and our silences even more so. The words whispered between us in silence fire my dreams with a passion unlike any I have ever felt. *You* interest me. All of you. Can you not see that?"

She chuckled, his flattering words not lost on her, though she was determined not to give in to the temptations on offer. She took another drink, even the wine tasting of salt this evening, her thirst going unquenched. "You flatter me, my liege, and were I not a queen, I might be tempted. But I must think of my people first, and to that end, I must take my leave of you. I depart early in the morning, and have a long journey ahead." She rose, as did all those gathered. She turned slowly, addressing them all, stopping at Solomon. "I thank you all for the hospitality shown me during my visit. It has been a highly rewarding undertaking, and I look forward to sharing what I have learned in your great kingdom with my people when I return."

She bowed deeply, the room following suit, along with Solomon, though the king merely nodded. He held out his hand and she took it. He led her from the hall they were gathered in, and toward her chambers.

"You're certain I can't change your mind."

"I am, and I beg of you to respect my wishes on the matter."

He stopped, taking her hands in his and clasping them to his chest. "Of course, of course." He stared into her eyes, her heart beating a little faster. "I shall ask nothing of you again, as long as you ask nothing of me."

She smiled. "I sense you are playing games with me yet again."

7

He chuckled, his smile intoxicating. "You know me too well, Makeda, my love." He leaned in closer, his lips almost pressed against her ear. "Take nothing of mine, and I shall take nothing of yours. You have my word." She was about to respond when he continued. "But should you take anything of mine this night, I will consider it your blessing for me to take anything of yours that I desire."

She patted him on the chest. "You are a clever man, and I fear there is a trick hidden in there somewhere, but fine, I agree. You have my word as well. After all, I am to bed now, then I depart in the morning." She stepped back and bowed. "Goodnight, my good king."

She entered her bedchambers, her guards closing the doors behind her. Her chambermaids made quick work of removing her clothes and jewelry, her ablutions swift and efficient. She dismissed them with a flick of her wrist and dropped into a deep, satisfying sleep within moments.

Makeda awoke with a start, sitting upright in her bed. She looked about for what had woken her, but found nothing. Nothing beyond an unquenchable thirst. As her eyes adjusted, she surveyed the room for a jug of water to satisfy her thirst, and froze. There were dozens surrounding her bed.

Those weren't there before.

The only explanation she could think of was that her servants had provided them after she fell asleep.

But why so many?

It made no sense.

She reached for the nearest jug, finding it heavy with liquid, and picked up a cup that sat beside it. She filled the cup and raised it to her lips.

A throat cleared and she flinched, her heart slamming as she spun toward the sound.

"Who dares enter my chambers without permission?"

Her voice was firm, brimming with authority, betraying none of the terror she felt at this moment.

"It is I, your king."

She relaxed, though only slightly, as she recognized Solomon's voice. Why was he here, in the middle of the night, watching her sleep? The invasion of her privacy was unconscionable, and never would have been tolerated if she were back home. "Then I ask *you*, why are you in my chambers without permission?"

He rose, his form silhouetted by the moonlight pouring through the windows. "I'm merely here to make certain you obey the oath you made to me."

She looked askance at him as she struggled to determine what it was the impetuous man was talking about, when she remembered her final words of the evening.

She peeled her tongue off the roof of her dry mouth. "I have taken nothing of yours."

He rounded the bed, gesturing at the cup in her hand. "That water is mine, and you are about to drink it."

Her eyes widened and her head tilted forward slightly, incredulous at his words. "Surely you are not serious."

"I am always serious when it comes to oaths made to me."

She shook her head, her thirst demanding satisfaction. "Forget the oath. Just let me drink."

"You are always free to make your own decisions."

She gulped down the precious water, refilling her cup several times as she sated the demand before returning the jug and cup where she found them. She turned to Solomon. "Now, if you would, please leave. I have a long journey ahead of me."

He shook his head, instead stepping closer. "You have broken your oath."

"It was a silly one, and you know it."

He grabbed her by the shoulders and spun her around, her back now facing him. "I told you that if you took anything of mine, I would consider it your blessing for me to take anything of yours I wanted."

He pressed against her and she could feel his desire. A wave of fear washed over her. "But...surely this was all in jest!"

He shoved her shoulders, bending her onto the bed as he lifted her robe. "Oaths are never something to be taken lightly."

"Please, I beg of you, don't do this."

"I am your king, and you have violated your sworn oath. And now I take that which you have offered in return."

And with one swift stroke, that which she had been saving for her wedding night was taken by a man she had thought wise and honest, instead revealing to her that both wisdom and carriage meant nothing to men of ultimate power.

Yet she didn't cry out for her guards, for the shame of it would be too great.

Instead, she cried into her bedding, biting down on her knuckle, and swore should she ever make it home, she would never again leave the sanctuary that was her kingdom, where no one would dare violate their queen such as this man.

King Solomon of the Israelites.

Ethiopia

Present Day, One Week Earlier

"Careful, brothers, remember how old it is."

Grunts were the only replies as the twelve men, much younger than Father Abune Amanuel, though still closer to middle age than their teens, strained to lift that which had been under their protection their entire lives, and for three thousand years before any of them had been born. It was a duty handed down over too many generations to count, though the Kebra Nagast did attempt to document much of it.

It was the history of the Ethiopian people, descended from the Queen of Sheba herself, and her illegitimate son, Menelik.

And he was responsible for their task today, millennia later.

The ancient relic was lifted from its platform, a seasonal event that saw it transferred from one secret location to another, and replaced with a fake, created with exacting precision that only an expert could tell the truth.

Something snapped.

Gasps and cries echoed in the small chamber as one side of the relic dropped toward the floor, the others quickly lowering the opposite side before the ancient vessel tumbled over, spilling its holy contents.

Father Amanuel lunged forward, his hands in front of him, hoping to hold the cover in place should it slip, then leaped back in horror as he realized that would involve touching it, something to be avoided if at all possible.

Or at the very least, vigorously discouraged.

Fortunately, the men at each of the four corners managed to safely return the relic to its resting place, everyone stepping away to catch their breath and stare at the pole that had just snapped after three thousand years of holding strong.

"What do we do now?" asked Harka, a trusted companion of many decades. "We can't carry it like this, and it's never to be touched except by the poles."

Father Amanuel frowned as he paced around their charge, inspecting it for any other damage, and happily finding none. "It is starting to finally show its age."

Harka grunted. "It's been showing its age for centuries, if not longer. It's finally *giving in* to its age."

Amanuel nodded. "You're right. Something must be done."

"Like what?"

"This is the most precious gift to mankind ever granted us by God. It must be preserved."

"But no one is allowed to see it!"

Amanuel sat on the floor, cross-legged, the others joining him in a circle. "Science is the answer."

"What do you mean?"

"I've read of how museums around the world control the air so that the objects are preserved. It's science far beyond me, but we need this type of technology if we're going to have any hope of preventing further damage."

"Science means scientists. That means outsiders."

"Unfortunately, yes."

"What about the Vatican? They have scientists."

Amanuel vehemently shook his head. "Never. They'll simply take it from us. They can never know we have it. Let them think we're fools, con artists hoping to deceive. Their arrogance has worked well for us so far. I see no reason to risk that now."

"Then who?"

"We need someone with expertise in preserving ancient things."

Harka shook his head. "I wouldn't even know what that is called. An archaeologist?"

They all paused, staring at each other as smiles spread.

Harka looked at Amanuel, his eyes wide. "Are you thinking what I'm thinking?"

"I believe so."

"But who will go?"

Amanuel drew a deep breath. "This is something that must be done in person. I'll go."

"But you're the Keeper! You've never left Ethiopia in your entire life! You don't know what it's like out there!"

Amanuel chuckled. "Do any of us?"

Harka frowned. "You're right, of course."

Amanuel leaned over and patted his friend on the knee. "Worry not, my friend. God will be my guide. He is always watching over us."

Ethiopia

10ᵗʰ Century BC, 22 Years Later

"Why have you never told me of my father?"

Queen Makeda tensed, keeping her back to her son Menelik. The boy was no longer a boy. He was a man, a man who deserved the truth, no matter how disturbing, and shameful, it was.

Yet did he?

She had protected him from the truth for over twenty years. No one knew what had happened, not even her closest confidants.

It was something one simply didn't speak of.

Yet without the truth, the apparent virgin birth had become legend within her kingdom, and Menelik revered as a great future leader who would guide his people with wisdom and the blessing of the Jewish god she now worshipped, as did many after they heard what she had been taught in Jerusalem by the boy's father and his rabbis.

It had been this newfound faith that had helped her through the shocking discovery she was pregnant on the journey home, a fact she had kept hidden at first, but when it became impossible, had decided, stupidly she now realized, to deny any knowledge of how it had happened.

There were whispers in the corridors of the palace, of course, though none dared confront her with demands for the truth.

None except her beloved son.

"No, I haven't spoken of him."

Menelik rounded her chair and sat across from her. "Why is that? Is it true what they say?"

She regarded him. "And what is it they say?"

"That you were a virgin when I was born."

She pursed her lips. "Not exactly something to ask of one's mother, is it?"

Menelik flushed and turned his head, staring at a golden elephant that occupied the corner of the room, its tusks encrusted with jewels. "I suppose not."

"Do you believe the stories?"

He shrugged. "If it were true, that I have no father, then that must mean my father is a god, perhaps even the Jewish god. But if that were true, if I were a demigod, then shouldn't I feel different? Shouldn't I have some sort of power that others don't?"

She sighed, closing her eyes. "And if you were the son of a god, *the* son of God, what would you do with such power should you discover it?"

His eyes widened as he turned back toward her, her question clearly suggesting to him that his musings might indeed be true. "I would conquer our enemies, securing better lives for our people. I would protect us from those who would take what we have, and make certain our countrymen enjoyed bountiful harvests, many children, and freedom from the ravages of nature and man. I would rid our kingdom of the evil that lurks within."

"All noble intentions. I'm impressed."

"Thank you."

"But do you think that power like this should be entrusted to a mere mortal?"

"What do you mean?"

She took a drink, resting her cup on the arm of her chair, swirling its contents. "It is said that evil lurks in the hearts of *all* men. Do you not feel it within your own?"

He shook his head vehemently. "Never!"

She eyed him. "Never?"

He flushed again. "Well, perhaps at times. But only when I'm really angry."

"And do you forgive those that anger you?"

He nodded. "Yes."

"All the time?"

He grunted. "Usually."

"Which means they probably didn't truly deserve your anger, did they?"

He sighed. "Yes, mother, you're right, of course." He stared at her. "And your point?"

"My point is this: if you had the power of a god when you were filled with such rage, would you have used it to strike out at those you were angry with? Would you have done irreparable harm, perhaps even killed them?"

Menelik drew a long, deep breath, his chest swelling as he considered her words, his eyes widening slightly. He exhaled loudly. "I fear I might have."

She was pleased with his admission. "So, perhaps it is best that you are not blessed with the power of a god."

He chuckled. "I suppose not." He eyed her. "Is this your roundabout way of telling me my father isn't a god?"

She smiled at him. "Yes."

He leaped to his feet, his face bright. "Then you *do* know who my father is?"

She steeled herself for the revelation she was finally about to reveal, her mind made up that it was at last time someone knew the truth, and if not her son, then who? "Yes."

He rushed forward, dropping to his knees at her feet, taking her hands in his, almost knocking the cup from its perch. "Please, mother, tell me who it is!"

She drew a breath, then revealed the secret that had eaten away at her for over two decades. "King Solomon."

He fell backward, his eyes wide, his mouth agape. "The wise one you told me of? The king of the Israelites in Jerusalem?"

She nodded. "Yes."

"But how? I mean, why? I mean…" He pushed to his feet and paced in front of her, muttering to himself before finally stopping and facing her. "Please, tell me how this could be true?"

She inhaled through her nose, her heart pounding, her palms sweaty as memories of that night, memories she had tried, and failed, to bury for so long, flooded back. Her eyes glistened and her ever faithful son noticed, returning to his knees and taking her hands.

"You don't have to tell me, if doing so will cause you pain."

A tear rolled down her cheek and she reached out for him, caressing his face, a face too much like his father's, and a constant reminder of the pain and humiliation she had suffered so long ago.

A trauma that had her never taking a husband, never having another child, never enjoying the pleasures of the flesh again.

Her jaw squared and she shook her head. "No, you must know. It is time." She took a short breath then exhaled quickly, the words spilling out rapidly before she changed her mind. "On the night before I left Jerusalem, King Solomon tricked me into an oath that I was forced to break due to his treachery, and he then raped me."

Menelik's nostrils flared and his eyes shot wide as his entire body clenched with anger, his chest heaving at her words. "My father took…he took your…" He stood, growling with anger, his fists clenched as he resumed pacing. He punched his palm then stopped. "I'm going to kill him."

She wiped the tears from her face, shaking her head. "No, that could lead to war."

"I don't care. He must pay for what he has done."

She rose, reaching out and taking his clenched fists in hers. "It has been over twenty years. He may be dead."

"Word would have reached us."

She frowned, for the boy was right.

"I want to meet him. To tell him that I know what he has done, and that I want nothing to do with him."

She sighed. "That is your right, of course." She took his chin in her hand and forced him to look her in the eyes. "But you mustn't kill him. You mustn't start a war that could lead to the death of our people."

He glared at her for a moment, then his shoulders slumped. "Very well. Once again, as always, you're right."

She smiled, patting his cheek. "You're a smart boy."

"I get it from you."

If only that were true.

"When will you leave?"

"As soon as I can."

She headed for her bedchambers. "If you are determined to meet your father, then there is something I must give you."

Menelik followed her. "What?"

"Something that proves to Solomon who you are." She shivered. "Something he gave me after he was done with me."

Bole International Airport

Addis Ababa, Ethiopia

Present Day

"Father Amanuel is boarding now."

"Destination?"

Dawit Ganno frowned. "London."

"And our sources have no idea why he's going there?"

"None."

"I guess you're right, we have to know."

Ganno headed for the gate. "I've booked a ticket on the same flight."

"Isn't that risky? What if he recognizes you?"

Ganno smiled at the woman at the gate as he handed her his passport and boarding pass. "He's never met me. They've never met any of us. That's the entire point of being a secret order that no one knows about."

"He may not know what you do, but he might have seen you driving by."

Ganno grunted. "Then it will simply be a happy coincidence, and nothing else will be said beyond pleasantries." He bowed slightly at the return of his documents and headed for the jetway. "And when I return, we will discuss my previous desire to have more of our members abroad. To think we have no one in England is ridiculous. This should be a phone call, not a flight."

"You're right, of course. But it's expensive to keep people around the world. Our man in the United States costs us handsomely."

Ganno sighed. His brother was right, and it was why the idea had been dropped after they had sent one of their own to New York City over a decade ago. When the bills started pouring in, they realized they simply didn't have the money for too many of these types of operatives. For now, they had one in Jerusalem, one in Rome, and one in New York City. That was it.

And it was already too expensive.

"Do you think he's going to reveal the secret?"

Ganno frowned. "I hope not, but something is going on. He's never left the country. No Keeper has."

"And if he does? What will you do?"

"If I think he's revealed the secret to anyone, I'll do what must be done."

"You mean kill him."

Ganno's frown deepened. "If necessary, though hopefully only those he tells. The secret must be preserved."

"Of course."

"Praise be to Menelik and Tamrin, and to our Lord, Jesus Christ."

23

Royal Palace of King Solomon

Jerusalem, Kingdom of Israel

10th Century BC

As Menelik's father spoke to those gathered, he absentmindedly spun the ring his mother had given him before his departure. His initial encounter hadn't gone as planned. He had intended to announce who he was then demand retribution for what King Solomon had done to his mother. Instead, the moment he had shown the man the ring given to his mother the night of her rape, Menelik had been embraced, genuine tears rushing down the cheeks of the man he had grown to hate over his long journey to Jerusalem.

Solomon had given him no time to spew the vitriolic denunciation Menelik had rehearsed during his voyage, and instead had announced to those gathered that his son had returned to him, and that it was a great day for the kingdom. He was peppered with questions with little if any time given for him to respond, and praise was heaped upon his mother, as if the rape had never occurred, or had been completely forgotten.

Or to Solomon, it never was rape.

He hadn't known how to react.

His father had turned out to not be the monster he had imagined, but instead an incredibly charismatic, captivating man. Intelligent, articulate, immaculate. His people both respected him and genuinely liked him, though he knew from his mother's court that facades were always on display in her presence.

One never made one's regent aware of any ill will.

And before that first night was through, Menelik was ashamed to admit he had been won over by the man. Not completely, but enough to delay any public humiliation he had planned.

And as the days progressed, and no opportune moment was found to confront the man, it became clear his father was incredibly pleased with his return.

"I want you to stay."

Menelik spun the ring again, still not used to wearing it, the pure gold, jewel-encrusted creation a constant reminder of his mother's betrayal. Solomon had raped her, then convinced he had impregnated her, given her the ring before her departure so when his son returned, Solomon would know it was him.

The ring had done its job, giving him access to Solomon within minutes of his arrival, the large royal procession also greasing the wheels. But the moment the ring had been spotted, Solomon's demeanor had changed from curiosity to, from all outward appearances, love for a son long lost.

"I must return home to my people."

"Your mother is a capable woman. She can take care of them."

"For now, yes, but in time it will be my job to lead my people."

Solomon motioned for him to sit closer to him, and Menelik complied. "And you will. I want you to remain and be my heir. Your kingdom will unite with mine, guaranteeing your people's protection."

Menelik regarded his father for a moment, then shook his head. "It is too far for you to offer any type of protection."

Solomon smiled. "You truly are a leader. Your first concern is your people, rather than the wealth and power I have just offered you." He gripped Menelik's shoulder, squeezing it. "You indeed are my son."

Menelik shoved his emotions deep, still reluctant to give into the charms of the man, but unsure of what he should do. He had no intentions of staying, no intentions of becoming king of a people he knew little about. He had been taught the language by scholars brought to the kingdom at the behest of his mother, her insistence he learn a language from a foreign land perhaps the first clue he had missed as to his origins.

Yet despite the fact he could converse comfortably with those around him, and despite the fact he worshipped their god—though perhaps without the same fervor—he felt as if he were an outsider.

And he had little doubt these people would never welcome a king whose bloodline wasn't entirely Jewish.

Solomon rose and beckoned for him to follow. "Come, I have something to show you that might change your mind."

Menelik hastened to catch up to his father, the old man still fleet of foot. "What?"

"Something very old. Very ancient." His father lowered his voice. "And very powerful."

Menelik's eyes widened slightly, intrigued at the gravitas conveyed by his father's words. "Powerful?"

Solomon nodded as they left the palace walls and made for the temple, the king's personal guard, as well as Menelik's, rushing to clear the way. "Yes. With it, my armies wield the power of God Himself."

Menelik eyed him skeptically, not one to believe in the power of talismans or the like. "And just what power does this…thing, wield, that could buttress an army?"

They entered the impressive structure, shown to him earlier in his visit, the guards clearing out the worshippers as they passed through the public area and into the back, down a set of winding stairs, the only light now provided by torches held by sconces mounted to the ancient walls. Solomon led him down a long hallway where an impressive, carved door stood, two guards on either side.

With a flick of his wrist, Solomon ordered the doors opened, the guards immediately granting them entrance.

And what Menelik saw had his jaw dropping as he came to a halt, the doors closing behind him. "What is it?"

"This, my son, is the source of our power. It is what gives us direct access to God, not only to his counsel, but his power as well. With this at the head of my army, no one can defeat us." He turned to Menelik. "And *this* is why I can guarantee your kingdom's security from such a great distance. Should anyone threaten you, I can send but a small contingent and defeat any enemy."

Menelik stared at the chest that stood in front of him, the craftsmanship that had gone into its construction impressive, the sheer amount of gold indicative of the value placed upon its significance. He rounded the chest, supported by four gold-plated feet, two poles, wrapped with gold, held on either side by rings of gold attached to the feet, obviously used to carry the creation, perhaps by Solomon's armies.

He paused, his heart hammering at the sight of two winged creatures, bowing toward the center, each with their wings outstretched, the reverence shown to whatever this represented evident.

His eyes narrowed as he realized that this chest did indeed have a top that appeared to be removable. "What does it contain?"

"The power and glory of God."

Menelik regarded his father. "And that is?"

Solomon smiled. "It contains several things, the most important of which are the original stone tablets containing the commandments we live by, given by God to Moses so long ago."

Menelik nodded slowly as he resumed his circuit around the impressive artifact. "How does it work?"

Solomon shook his head. "That, I cannot say, except that when carried before our armies, no one has been able to defeat us."

"But what does it *do*? I mean, it must *do* something in order to defeat an army."

"It is forbidden to speak of such things. Our most holy of men carry it ahead of our army, out of sight of us mere mortals, and when we arrive, we find our enemies slain." Solomon shuddered. "Even I dare not question its power."

The hair on the back of Menelik's neck stood, a shiver rushing over his body as Solomon's words, and tone, sank in. Could this chest truly contain the power of the Jewish god? Could it indeed protect his kingdom from any threats? And if it could, would the price for access to its protection mean he would be forced to remain here, never again to see his mother and his people?

He reached out to touch it, the urge irresistible, when Solomon grabbed his hand with an iron grip.

"It must never be touched!"

Menelik flushed, as if an admonished child, then stepped backward. "Then how do you carry it into battle?"

Solomon released his grip, then patted one of the two poles. "With these. These are the only part of the Ark that should be touched by man."

Menelik frowned. "Then how do you know what is inside?"

Solomon chuckled. "I have faith."

Menelik nodded. "What did you call it? An ark?"

"It is the Ark of the Covenant, and with it, my people can never be defeated." He put a hand on Menelik's shoulder. "Nor can yours."

London, England

Present Day

Dawit Ganno watched as the taxi pulled over, Father Amanuel climbing out moments later before ascending a set of steps. A man answered the door, and the elderly priest entered, as if expected. He turned to his driver, a local man with Ethiopian ties, provided in advance by the Ethiopian Friendship Center.

An organization that knew nothing of the order, or their mission.

"What address is that?"

The driver pointed at the GPS. "It's right there. Number"—he peered out the window, squinting against the dark and the heavy rain—"1502."

"Can you get me the name of who lives there?"

His driver eyed him with suspicion. "Why? Are you some sort of copper?"

"Yes."

The lie satisfied the young man, and he pulled out his phone, something far fancier than his own, and began tapping away at it. Moments later, he held it up. "Looks like some bloke named Ullendorff."

Ganno's heart fluttered at the name, his eyes widening. It had never occurred to him that Father Amanuel might visit the one man who knew the secret that shouldn't.

"Do you know the guy?"

Ganno ignored the question. It didn't make sense. Lieutenant Ullendorff had seen the relic in World War Two, and it was unlikely he was alive today.

He turned to the driver. "How old would you say the man was that answered the door?"

The driver shrugged. "I don't know. Sixties?"

"That's what I thought as well."

"Is he who you're looking for?"

"I'm not sure." He nodded toward the phone. "Can you bring up an obituary on a Lieutenant Ullendorff?"

The driver's eyebrows rose, but he complied, and moments later he was reading the highlights, the man having died in 2011, leaving a son behind. "That must be the son's house."

Ganno pursed his lips, unsure of what to do. Lieutenant Ullendorff knew their secret through chance. He had gone public with it, then recanted, thanks to efforts by the Keepers and Ganno's ancestors. It was likely the son knew the story, though didn't believe it.

Yet the question remained.

What possible business could Father Amanuel have with the son of the one man they had left alive over seventy years ago?

"Thank you for agreeing to see me on such short notice."

Steven Ullendorff smiled, taking Father Amanuel's coat and hanging it up. "It's my pleasure, Father. It's not every day one gets a phone call from a priest requesting an audience."

Ullendorff led him into a humble sitting room, his wife, already introduced at the door, bringing in a tea service. Poured, he clasped the cup with both hands, its warmth welcome, the chill and damp of an English evening something he had never experienced. He took a sip and smiled his appreciation at Mrs. Ullendorff, then dashed her hopes of an entertaining interlude.

"May we speak alone, Mr. Ullendorff. I'm afraid this is a very private matter."

Ullendorff's eyes widened and he exchanged a glance with his wife. "A private matter? With you? No offense, Father, but, umm, you're not exactly from these parts. What possible business could we have?"

"It's regarding your father."

His eyes widened further, a shaky nod escaping before he ushered his protesting wife up the stairs.

"I'm sorry about that, Mr. Ullendorff, but it was necessary." Amanuel lowered his voice. "Did your father ever tell you about his time in Ethiopia?"

Ullendorff shook his head. "No, beyond that he was there during the war." His eyes narrowed. "Why, did something happen while he was there?"

Relief swept over Amanuel at the news. The elder Ullendorff had kept his promise, though only after being reminded of the original broken oath made to a layman years ago. Amanuel hadn't been involved, though whatever had been said was enough for the man to later recant, at great risk to his reputation, preserving the secret of a discovery that could have made him famous the world over.

Perhaps he was simply a good man.

He looked about the room, noting several texts displayed with prominence, dealing with what appeared to be archaeology, with the son's name on the cover. "I see you followed in your father's footsteps."

"Yes, in part. Obviously, I chose archaeology as my profession, not the military, whereas my father had no choice at the time but to put his ambitions aside."

Amanuel nodded slowly. "In war, much is demanded of us. But it is your archaeology expertise that I have a need for."

Ullendorff chuckled, shaking his head. "I'm afraid I retired a few years ago, Father, but I'm happy to help in any way I can. What do you want to know?"

"We have something very old that needs to be preserved before it's too late."

Ullendorff laughed. "Let me guess, the Ark of the Covenant?"

Amanuel managed to keep a straight face, though his pulse pounded with the implications of the man's words.

"Don't tell me you believe the lies that were written about my father."

Amanuel calmed slightly. "Lies?"

"Yes, about how he was shown the Ark when he was in Ethiopia during the war?"

Amanuel knew the story well. Every Keeper did. It served as a warning to all who undertook the honor of protecting the greatest of all secrets. During the war, a Keeper had left his post, leaving a layman behind to guard the Ark. When a British military unit arrived on patrol, led by Lieutenant Ullendorff, he insisted on seeing inside the church carved into the ground, a church of such construction something the lieutenant had never seen before.

And the layman had allowed it, terrified of the armed men.

And the layman had confirmed it was the Ark of the Covenant that sat inside.

When the breach had been discovered, after the war, and after the lieutenant had already gone public, many things had been changed in their procedures so it could never happen again.

Fortunately, it had happened so long ago, before the Internet had existed, that the incident was forgotten, and was now merely a conspiracy theory they were happy to exploit.

Amanuel smiled at Ullendorff and chuckled. "No, not the Ark, however something equally precious to us. It is very old, and time and nature have taken their toll. We must preserve it, and were hoping you might know how."

Ullendorff shook his head. "I'm not an expert in preservation, and besides, I'm retired."

Amanuel frowned, leaning back in his chair. "Can you recommend someone? Someone who can be trusted to not only do the job well, but keep it a secret?"

Ullendorff eyed him. "For a priest, you really are concerned with your secrets, aren't you?"

Amanuel smiled, waving his hand. "I come from a dangerous part of the world, where many would destroy anything they considered blasphemous."

Ullendorff grunted, his head bobbing. "I hear ya. Well, I worked out of the British Museum. The head of archaeology there was Professor Laura Palmer. She was excellent, with a good reputation, though she did have some whacky theories about those crystal skulls. I'd contact her. She would definitely have the expertise, and I knew her for years. She's young—at least compared to me—but extremely honest. She's probably exactly what you're looking for."

"Professor Laura Palmer, was it?" Ullendorff nodded and Amanuel wrote down the name. "Thank you for your time." He rose and bowed slightly. "I must be going, I've taken enough of your evening." He waved his notepad before tucking it into his robes. "Thank you for this." He shuffled for the door, then Ullendorff helped him into his coat. "Thank you, my son." He lowered his voice. "Tell no one of my visit. Should the wrong people know I was here, meeting with an archaeologist, they might think my church back home had something worth stealing."

Ullendorff's jaw squared. "Of course, Father, your secret is safe with me."

Royal Palace of King Solomon

Jerusalem, Kingdom of Israel

10th Century BC

Saul stood at the front of the gathered crowd of Jerusalem's ruling elite. His favored position had been occupied for as long as he had been a member of this court, the same honor bestowed upon his father, and his father's father. He was loyal to his king, though the spectacle on display enraged him to his core.

A king, a Jewish king, fawning over a half-breed bastard convert from a foreign land, with the audacity to suggest he should inherit the throne and lead the Israelites upon his death.

It was outrageous, and if pursued, could lead to the end of King Solomon, no matter how loyal his subjects were.

The King's desires would never be permitted.

Solomon had just spent the last ten minutes exalting his son, the young man, to his credit, seeming embarrassed by the words of praise

36

heaped upon him. And when Solomon revealed he had shown this Menelik their holiest of relics, a relic even Saul had never laid eyes upon, a collective gasp of horror and outrage had swept the court, the revulsion at the revelation ignored as Solomon droned on.

If he's revealed the source of our power, of our link to God, then Menelik may have been swayed.

"But, alas, even I haven't been able to persuade my son to stay among us. As you know, I have asked him to stay, to become my heir"—again disgruntled grumblings filled the room—"however he has decided to return home to help his people, continuing the exchange of knowledge begun with his mother, Queen Makeda." Solomon paused, his eyes staring into the distance, as if into the past. "To that end, I have decided that to help my son's kingdom prosper, and to achieve the greatness we have in the name of the one true God, I hereby decree that the firstborn of all noble and rabbinical families shall accompany my son on his journey home, to assist him in the betterment of his kingdom."

Saul's jaw dropped and his eyes widened as he stared at his king, dumbfounded. Questions rippled through those gathered, many uncertain they had heard Solomon correctly, and once their fears had been confirmed, outrage tore through the room, the sense of open revolt causing the guards surrounding the room to shift in their places, uncertain of what to do.

"This is outrageous!" cried Saul, stepping forward, his privileged position giving him a direct line of sight to the king who would betray them all over a boy he barely knew. "This is unacceptable! I will *not* send my son Jonathan with this child to Africa! How dare you ask this of us?

We have served you loyally for decades, and you betray us like this! It is unconscionable!"

Fists pumped the air as others edged forward, emboldened by his tirade, the guards rushing to fill the narrowing gap between Solomon and his irate subjects.

Yet Solomon didn't react.

Though his son did.

With fear and embarrassment.

Solomon rose, raising a hand, his expression calm, the room eventually settling to hear what was about to be said. Saul's heart pounded and sweat trickled down his back, as the next words could mean the end of his life for having challenged his king.

"Anyone whose firstborn isn't in the courtyard in two days' time, will be executed along with their son."

Saul pressed his luck, stepping forward again, a spear immediately blocking his path. "How can you do this, how can you put the future of Jerusalem, the future of our people, at risk like this? How can you weaken our kingdom by sending away our best and brightest?"

Solomon finally acknowledged him. "They will be gone only for as long as they are needed."

Though it was a small concession, it wasn't enough, yet he knew there would be no further discussion of the matter. This wasn't a negotiation. Solomon had made up his mind, and when he did, there was simply no changing it. He was about to lose his son to the unknown continent, for how long he didn't know, with dangers he could only imagine.

Most likely, the future of the Jewish people, its cherished sons, would never return.

"My king," he said, calming his voice, stepping slightly closer, his head bowed in reverence. "Please, if we are to send our sons as you ask, let them take the Ark of the Covenant with them so that they may be protected by the power of God from harm."

Murmurs of agreement washed over the room, his idea clearly agreeable to all the fathers gathered.

"Out of the question."

Solomon spun on his heel and left the hall, the court erupting in rage the moment he was out of sight though not out of earshot.

"What are we going to do?" asked Benjamin, the head of another noble family that traced its lineage back as far as Saul's did. "Are we going to stand for this?"

Saul watched Menelik rush from the chamber after his father, his shoulders rounded, his head down.

He never asked for this, nor does he want it.

"What can we do?" he replied, shaking his head. "Challenge our king? He'll have us all put to death."

"Surely if we all unite as one, he'll change his mind."

Saul shook his head. "This is Solomon we're speaking of."

Benjamin sighed, throwing up his hands in frustration as a group gathered around them, clusters of loud conversations filling the hall. "Then we are to capitulate? To give up our firstborn on this ridiculous venture? All for some bastard son from a backwater kingdom?"

There were grumblings, though no one said anything, instead, all eyes turning to Saul, the most senior among them. He thought for a moment, moving past the useless thoughts of how to keep his son here in Jerusalem, and instead focusing on how to protect him while he was away, and no matter how large a contingent of soldiers they might muster to accompany their brave sons, he could think of only one way to guarantee their safety.

He stared at the others, and was about to tell them his plan, when he decided against it.

For it would take only one to betray him, and it would mean certain death.

Instead, he let his shoulders sag. "I can think of nothing, but to obey our king."

The disappointment of those gathered was obvious, and he broke from the group, heading home, his outrageous plan already weaving itself together.

A plan that had to succeed, but could condemn him for eternity should it go wrong.

For stealing the Ark of the Covenant was surely an act against God Himself.

Acton/Palmer Residence

St. Paul, Maryland

Present Day

"Do these pants make me look fat?"

Professor James Acton's eyebrows shot up, every alarm bell in the male system going off. "Huh?" was the best he could manage.

"These pants, the way they flare at the top. I think they make me look fat."

Acton tried to hide his awareness of the mantrap set for him, instead scratching his chin and carefully regarding his wife, Archaeology Professor Laura Palmer, as she turned in front of him.

"Well?"

"I think they accentuate your figure. You look fantastic."

"Accentuate? As in make something appear more prominent. Like my hips?"

Sir Mix-a-Lot's Baby Got Back came to mind, but he bit his tongue. He stabbed an accusatory finger at her. "You're trying to get me in trouble."

She grinned and stepped out of the pants, throwing them at him as he lounged on the bed, reading some essays his students had turned in, too many a disappointment, something he had come to expect from first-years. They now came out of high school lacking the basics, and too many had no concept of attribution, instead taking entire passages from the work of others and inserting them in their own work as if it were theirs.

At least now there was software to catch much of it, though he had only flunked a few who turned in entire papers bought from students at other schools. The others, he showed how to create a bibliography, then forced them to rewrite the paper using one.

Ignorance shouldn't kill your future, but outright copying? Every time.

"How about you put those papers aside, Professor, and make your wife feel like a woman."

Acton grinned, tossing the printouts onto the floor and slipping out of his pants in one swift motion. "Ta-da!"

Laura threw her head back, laughing. "Is that your version of pulling a rabbit out of a hat?"

"It does tricks! Watch!"

The doorbell rang.

They both growled.

Acton reached over and grabbed his phone, the doorbell camera automatically sending him a live feed of who was there. His eyebrows shot up. "Now there's something you don't see every day."

"Who is it?"

He tossed the phone toward the end of the bed as he rolled out of it, slipping his pants back on. "Is that what I think it is?"

"A priest on our doorstep? Yes."

"No, I mean—"

The doorbell rang again, the elderly man looking about as if he had no idea he was on camera. Laura activated the speaker using the phone. "One moment, please."

It startled the man, Laura grinning as she turned the phone around for Acton to see. "Poor guy, judging from where he's from, he's probably never seen anything like this smart home stuff." He headed for the door, Laura stumbling back into her flared pants, both presentable by the time he opened the door.

"Yes?"

The priest stared at him for a moment, flustered, then spotted Laura. "Are you Professor Palmer? Professor Laura Palmer?"

She nodded and Acton ceded his position. "I am. And you are?"

"I am Father Amanuel. I come to you on an urgent matter. You were recommended to me by Professor Ullendorff, formerly of the British Museum."

Laura's face brightened in recognition. "Steven Ullendorff? I know him well. It's been some time though since I've seen him." She invited the old man inside. "Please, come in. You look exhausted."

And he did. The man's movements were slow, his skin pale, his eyes bloodshot with circles under them. Laura led him into the living room and guided him to their most comfortable chair. "Can I get you anything?"

"Water would be wonderful."

Acton headed for the kitchen, open to the living room, and retrieved a glass, filling it with ice and filtered water from the fridge. He offered it to the man, who took a sip gratefully. He smiled.

"Ice cubes! Now there's a rare treat."

They both took seats opposite Father Amanuel, Laura taking the lead. "So, Father, what is it I can do for you?"

"Professor Ullendorff told me you are an expert in the preservation of ancient artifacts."

"I am. What is it you need preserved?"

"I cannot say, but it is very important that it be protected. It is starting to deteriorate, and I'm not sure how much longer it has if we don't take immediate action."

"How old is it?"

Amanuel hesitated, as if the age might reveal what it was. "Thousands of years."

Acton whistled. "What is it made of?"

"Gold and wood."

Laura's head bobbed. "Let me guess, the gold is fine, but the wood is starting to crack."

"Exactly. I think the air is simply too dry."

"You'll need to control the environment it's in for temperature and humidity, and air purity, of course. We could create a room that you could keep it in. That would preserve it, and allow people to see it, depending on the design."

Amanuel shook his head. "No, that won't do. We need to be able to move it."

Laura's eyes widened slightly. "Well, I'd advise against that. Any movement could damage it further should it not be done properly."

Amanuel frowned. "I'm afraid that isn't an option. We must be able to move it."

"How often?"

"Four times a year, more should it become necessary."

Acton regarded the man, Amanuel clearly nervous about something. "And why might it become necessary?"

Amanuel drew a long breath, turning to Acton. "I really can't say. What I need is something that the object can be placed inside, that is portable. Something a dozen men, for example, could carry, when necessary. It can't be much bigger than the object itself, otherwise it won't fit out the door. Can you design something like this?"

Laura nodded. "Of course, it should be quite easy. When we install it, we can adjust everything based upon the condition of the object, and the environmental conditions of the area."

Amanuel shook his head. "No, I just need you to design it, with instructions on how to build it. You can't see the object."

Laura frowned. "I'm afraid it doesn't work that way, Father. If you want us to do this properly, then we have to do it in person. There's no other way, otherwise you're just wasting your time and money."

It was clear this wasn't what Amanuel wanted to hear, his shoulders sagging, his head drooping.

He's so tired.

Acton leaned forward, delivering his words as calmly and soothingly as possible. "Father, if what you want to preserve is so important, you need the work done properly, agreed?"

The old man sighed, but nodded. "Yes."

"And it's clear the location and identity of the object must be kept secret."

A more emphatic nod.

"Then you have nothing to worry about. We can sign any non-disclosure agreements you want, and you'll have our word we won't tell anyone."

Laura agreed. "No one. No friends or colleagues. No priests." She smiled and Amanuel brightened slightly.

"So, I have your word that you will tell no one?"

"Absolutely," said Laura.

"And we'll sign anything you want."

Amanuel shook his head. "Paper is worthless. But a man's word, or a woman's, can be everything, if it is the right man or woman." He regarded them both for a moment. "I feel God has sent me to the right people." He smiled. "We have an agreement."

Laura leaned forward, extending a hand, and Amanuel shook it, Acton doing the same.

"So, what makes this so valuable that it needs to be kept a secret?"

Amanuel frowned. "Where I am from, there are too many people who would steal or destroy what we hold so dear." He took a sip of his water, swirling the contents and smiling slightly at the clinking of the ice cubes. "How long will it take for you to gather what you need?"

Laura picked up her iPad from the table, quickly typing out some notes. "Well, because you want it to be portable, it actually makes the process much easier, since we're not building or adapting a room. I'm assuming since it's small enough to be carried, that we're not talking something large like a boat."

Amanuel shook his head and removed a piece of paper from his pocket. "No. These are the precise measurements from end to end, top to bottom, as well as its estimated weight."

Laura entered the measurements. "Well, that's definitely easily self-contained. Do you have a steady supply of electricity?"

Amanuel sighed. "Unfortunately, only at some locations it will be kept, and I would never call anything steady where I am from."

"Then you'll need a generator. Diesel?"

Amanuel nodded. "Yes, we have access to plenty of diesel."

"What about solar?"

Amanuel shook his head. "Too conspicuous. People would wonder why a church had solar panels. A generator can be hidden, and excused."

"And you said it was built from gold and wood."

"Yes."

"Well, the gold obviously isn't a problem, as long as everything is on a stable platform to prevent any damage from torsion. The wood, if we can keep everything stable and the environment within the unit stable, shouldn't be a problem either." She waved the tablet. "I'll put the specs together tonight, and give you a price in the morning. It will be steep, but not too crazy. We'll do the work for free—"

Amanuel's eyes widened. "For free?"

Laura smiled. "We have no need of money, Father. Where are you staying?"

"I'm returning immediately. I've been away for too long."

"Then where can we send everything?"

Amanuel fished a piece of paper from his pocket, pushing it across the table toward Laura. "All my contact information is there. How long do you think it will take?"

Laura shrugged. "Not long at all. A day or two. This is pretty standard stuff. The trick is knowing how to put it all together, then what the correct settings are." She grinned. "It's all in the calibration."

Acton picked up the piece of paper, his eyebrows rising slightly. "Casablanca?" He eyed the priest for a moment. "Don't you mean Addis Ababa?"

Amanuel's jaw dropped. "How-how do you know that?"

Acton smiled slightly. "We're archaeologists and anthropologists. I can tell just by looking at you and listening to your accent what part of Africa you're from. This will go a lot quicker if you just tell us the truth."

Amanuel stared at him blankly for a moment, then sighed. "You're correct, of course. The ultimate destination for your equipment is Ethiopia."

A smile spread on Acton's face. "And the object you need us to preserve is the Ark of the Covenant."

Amanuel stared at Acton in horror, all strength failing him. He slumped in his chair and Acton leaped forward, supporting him by the shoulder.

"Breathe, Father, breathe. There's nothing to be worried about."

Amanuel sucked in a breath, then another, and soon recovered, Acton handing him his water. He took several sips, his strength returning, before he nodded at the younger man. "I-I'm okay now." He stared at Acton. "What would make you say such a thing?"

Acton smiled gently, returning to his seat. "Well, you seem to forget you're dealing with experts."

Laura leaned closer to the priest. "The Bible gives the measurements of the Ark as two-and-a-half cubits by one-and-a-half by one-and-a-half. Add on the feet, the cover with cherubim, and the poles made of gold-clad acacia wood long enough for this *very* heavy object to be carried, and the measurements you gave are too close not to make one wonder when put into context."

"And what, umm, context is that?"

"Where you're from. Most archaeologists with an interest in Bible relics have heard the theory that the Ark was stolen by the son of King Solomon and the Queen of Sheba, or others with him, and taken to Ethiopia where it has been kept hidden until this day. The only thing is that most archaeologists also know that the story is a fraud, with dozens of churches in Ethiopia actually claiming to have the Ark, though none, conveniently, ever show it."

Acton raised a finger. "Except for one report from an amateur archaeologist after the war."

"Named...Ullendorff!" Laura's jaw dropped. "Was he Steven's father?"

Amanuel nodded. "He was."

She stared at the elderly man for a moment. "You're serious about this, aren't you? I mean, you're not asking us to preserve a fake. You're asking us to preserve the real thing."

"I was told you can be trusted."

"We can."

"And you will never repeat anything you have heard, or will see?"

"We won't."

"And you'll swear this before God?"

"We will."

Amanuel rose. "Then bring what you need to preserve what I have described to Ethiopia as soon as you can. Contact me with your itinerary, and your price. The money will be wired to your account by my people, and you will be met and transported to my church when you arrive. There, all will be revealed."

Acton rose, clearly excited. "You mean we'll get to see the Ark?"

Amanuel smiled slightly. "I said nothing of the sort. And I must stress this point again. You must tell *no one*. Should anyone find out, should anyone know of our meeting, we could all die."

Acton tensed. "Why?"

"There are those who would do anything to have what we possess, and they will stop at nothing to get it. If you value your lives, and those of your friends, you will tell no one anything. Understood?"

"Yes," they both echoed, the excitement on their faces waning.

"Good. I must leave at once. I've been gone for too long for them not to have noticed."

"Them?"

"Not your concern. Just remember what I said. Tell no one."

Corpo della Gendarmeria Office
Palazzo del Governatorato, Vatican City

Inspector General Mario Giasson of the Corps of Gendarmerie of Vatican City State wiped the sweat off his bald head with a handkerchief, cursing the failed air conditioning. It had been down for two days, each time it was declared fixed, the aging system dying minutes later.

It was time it was taken out back and shot, and everyone sent home.

Unfortunately, they were doing the work of God, and had to think of His needs, not their own. That was little comfort to those trapped in the heat, dozens of fans supplied by Facilities Management spread across the office, including one in his own, supplemented by several more he had brought from home.

His air conditioning worked fine, despite few of his neighbors owning a system.

It just wasn't a European thing.

Somebody cheered and he looked out at the office beyond his glass walls to see his staff rushing toward any vent they could find, cool air apparently once again flowing.

Yeah, but for how long?

He said a quick prayer for the skills of the repairmen and the health of the HVAC system, then rose, stepping over to a vent and enjoying the chill that rushed over his body.

Thank you, God.

Then it stopped.

And he growled, giving an eye to the Lord above, then immediately apologized.

He'll understand.

His phone rang and he grabbed the handset, returning to his seat, the momentary relief already forgotten. "Giasson."

"Hey, Mario, Jim Acton here."

Giasson smiled and leaned back in his chair, trying to recall the last time he had seen the American professor and his British wife, and whether bullets had been involved. "Jim, good to hear your voice. To what do I owe the pleasure?"

"I've got a question for you that I was hoping you could help me out on."

"I'll try."

"What can you tell me about a Father Abune Amanuel, working out of Ethiopia?"

Giasson's eyes narrowed. "Why?"

"I just need to know if he's legit."

"Is he Roman Catholic?"

"I'm guessing Ethiopian Orthodox."

Giasson frowned. "That makes it a little more difficult. Let me check." He brought up the personnel directory, entering the search parameters. Though they had complete records on their own priests, other offshoots relied more on records searches and voluntarily supplied lists by the other faiths. A result appeared, and Giasson smiled. "It's your lucky day, Jim. It's confirmed. Father Abune Amanuel, graduated from the Theological College of the Holy Trinity in Addis Ababa almost forty years ago, and is assigned to the Church of Saint Mary of Zion, though that might not be current." He leaned back in his chair. "What's this about?"

"I can't say, but if anyone calls asking about him or us, let me know. And make sure you tell them nothing."

Giasson leaned forward. "You're making me nervous."

Acton laughed. "Now why would you ever get nervous about me?"

Giasson grunted. "Because every time I've met you, I've been either shot or shot at."

"Good times!"

Giasson chuckled. "I'm not sure that's how I'd describe it." He became serious. "Jim, I don't know what you've got yourself involved in this time, but try not to get killed."

"We'll do our best. Talk to you soon, my friend."

"Au revoir."

The call ended and Giasson stared at the screen. This priest was obviously involved in whatever Acton was mixed up in. He opened his browser and searched the name, finding nothing of interest, and nothing referencing Father Amanuel correctly. He entered the name of the church and his jaw dropped.

Oh my God!

He clicked on the first link, quickly scanning the article, then backing out and reading the next.

It can't be!

Yet could it?

He reached for the phone then stopped.

You gave your word!

He closed his eyes, trying to steady his hammering heart.

But your primary obligation is to the Church. Isn't it?

He bowed his head, clasping his hands in front of him.

Lord, what do I do?

The First Temple

Jerusalem, Kingdom of Israel

10th Century BC

Saul strode with purpose, accompanied by his son and a dozen of the young man's most trusted friends, all about to be sent on Solomon's fool's errand. Above them, in the temple, the leaders of the kingdom were in prayer for the safe return of their firstborn sons.

But he had no time for that.

Though if anyone were to ask tomorrow if Saul had been in attendance, in his usual position of honor at the front of those gathered, the answer would be a resounding yes. For his trusted servant, of similar build and features, was wearing his clothes, and was surrounded by the fathers of the young men that accompanied them on their mission.

As he walked down the long hall toward the ornate doors at the end, the guards snapped to attention as they recognized him. It was unfortunate that it didn't matter, for there was only one solution to the problem of them knowing he was here instead of at worship overhead.

"Sir, I must ask what you are doing here?"

Saul came to a stop directly in front of the guards, clearly nervous, but not enough to defend themselves against the swift attack executed by his son and his friends, daggers plunged then twisted into the stomachs of the souls unfortunate enough to have the honor of guarding the Ark in these dark hours.

Saul opened the unlocked door, there no need for security beyond the ceremonial guard, for who would dare steal something that wasn't theirs to take?

For this was the property of God.

And it would remain so, for it would be used for God's work. If his son was to be sent to a faraway land to spread to the heathens of the unknown continent the word of God and the wisdom He had given the Jewish people, then this was indeed God's work, and he prayed he, and the few involved, would be forgiven for what they were about to do.

He stepped inside, the others dragging the bodies after him, then dropped to his knees as a rapturous sense of awe swept through him at the sight of the Ark, an object so beautiful, he gasped for breath as he finally realized it had been held.

"Father, we must act quickly."

Saul ignored his son for a moment, taking in what he had only dreamed of for so long, this manmade creation, built to the specifications provided by God, far more inspiring than he could possibly have imagined.

A tear rolled down his cheek, a moment of self-doubt entering his mind.

By what right do you do this?

"Father!"

Saul finally reacted to the hand shaking his shoulder, and stared up into the eyes of his beloved son.

He's why.

He nodded, pushing to his feet, flicking his wrist at the Ark. "Cover it, but be careful to touch nothing but the poles. You must never touch it. Remember that."

"Yes, Father."

A large cloth was cast over the gold plated creation, then his son and the others positioned themselves, lifting the Ark. Saul stared at the bodies of the innocent guards, saying a silent prayer, then led them out of the chamber, his heartbeat racing, the sudden sound of the doors closing behind him enough to make him flinch as he tried to steady his nerves.

He closed his eyes for a moment, begging God for forgiveness for what he had done.

Please stop us now, should you not approve.

He opened his eyes, finding their way still clear, and breathed a sigh of relief as they reached the top of the stairs, no one in sight, the prayer services continuing on the other side of the wall.

Thank you.

And within minutes, the Ark was loaded into the back of a waiting cart, covered in plain cloths, the horses led out by one of his servants, ignorant as to the cargo, with instructions to head out of town.

Where tomorrow, his son and his friends would collect it, and join the large caravan of Jerusalem's finest as it departed the only home most had ever known.

And entered the wilds of an untamed continent, without the armies of their brothers to protect them.

But with the power of God instead.

New York City, New York
Present Day

"He's on a flight back home now."

"You didn't come back with him?"

Ganno shook his head. Three led the Sons of Tamrin, and he was but one. That meant he had to answer to his brothers, even his youngest, Theodros. "No. He met with two archaeologists earlier today. I think he may have told them, though I can't be sure."

"What's your plan?"

"I'm going to continue to monitor them. See what they do, who they talk to."

"If they've been told, you know what must be done."

"Of course I do, brother. Remember, I'm the eldest. I've been doing this longer than you have."

Theodros chuckled. "*Two* years longer. Hardly anything to hold over my head."

Ganno smiled. "You'll always be my baby brother." He became serious. "If these professors have been told of the Ark's existence, their lives must be forfeit before they tell anyone else. I'm going to need help, though. Tell Asrat to contact me immediately."

"Consider it done. Be safe, brother."

"Praise be to Menelik and Tamrin, and to our Lord, Jesus Christ."

Bedford Park, New York City

Asrat Fida stared at the message on his phone, his heart pounding, a smile spreading. It was a message he had never expected, not after so many years of waiting, so many years of isolation and boredom.

It was the day he had been waiting for.

This is my chance!

When he had volunteered to move to America and live here in case he was one day needed, he hadn't understood what that meant. He had always been poor. Most in Ethiopia were. But to be poor in a poor country was one thing, especially when surrounded by family and friends who suffered equally.

But here, in New York City, being poor was an entirely different experience. It meant near inhumane conditions in a rich country. He had no money to do anything but huddle in his hovel of an apartment in a rundown tenement in the Bronx. He had no money beyond the meager allowance sent to him monthly, certainly a princely sum in Ethiopia, but a pittance in America—nearly every penny consumed by rent, food, and a phone.

If it weren't for his phone, he'd have killed himself long ago. They had left him here for over a decade, with almost no word, and no indication of when he'd be allowed back home.

He feared they couldn't afford to bring him back.

Yet did he really want to go back? Life here was hard, though it was far more interesting than that back in Ethiopia. It could be violent here, dangerous, but if he kept to himself, and made sure he was in before dark, even the hellhole he lived in was fine. He had a cheap television he had found in the garbage years ago that picked up channels with its bent antennae, he had free wi-fi from neighbors who didn't understand basic Internet security, and he never worried about food or water.

If he thought about it, it wasn't that bad a life.

Certainly better than what he had left.

It was the loneliness that was killing him.

Stolen wi-fi allowed him to surf the web on his phone, or his laptop for more intensive work, but he rarely interacted with anyone. He had no social life, as he had no money. He supplemented his income with a part-time janitorial job, barely enough for the coffee habit he had developed, and the occasional treat. He hadn't been with a woman in years, and even that was when he had managed to scrape together enough money to pay for it, an experience he swore never to repeat for the shame of it.

He had no friends, kept to himself, and devoted most of his time to prayer and his assigned task: to learn everything he could about how to help the order, should it become necessary.

He now knew how to pick locks, override security systems, hack computers, plant listening devices, and more. He studied everything he could think of, and practiced whenever possible. He didn't consider himself an expert, though he was good enough, honing his skills by breaking into homes and apartments around the area, hacking their computers, then leaving, taking nothing that might alert anyone that he had been there.

He had a few close calls—the only excitement in his life—though had always escaped. He was good. Not the best, not an expert, but good enough for whatever the order might need him for.

And if Ganno were here, one of the leaders of the order, then something must be happening with the Ark.

And if something were happening with the Ark, then this might be the first chance in thousands of years for anyone to profit from it.

He smiled.

For he intended for that person to be him.

He pulled out his laptop and connected to the neighbor's wi-fi. He activated a Dark Web browser, initiating the first step of a plan he had been working on for years, once he had discovered what was possible thanks to his studying. He posted his message, carefully crafted, on a dark corner of the illicit Internet meant for collectors.

Collectors with absolutely no scruples.

And unimaginably deep pockets.

Pockets that could give him the life he deserved. The life he had never known possible until he arrived on the shores of his new home.

America.

Royal Palace of King Solomon

Jerusalem, Kingdom of Israel

10th Century BC

Saul's heart hammered as he joined the others gathered in the court, King Solomon's throne unoccupied despite the order to gather having been issued by him. The room was packed with both nobility and religious authorities, the guard far heavier than usual, as if Solomon expected trouble.

And it could mean only one thing.

His treachery had been discovered.

The fact he stood here among the others, however, told him Solomon had no idea he was involved. For if he did, Saul was certain he'd already be staked and crucified, his family slaughtered before his eyes while he suffered for his betrayal, an example for all to behold lest they think of crossing Solomon in the future.

The room fell silent as Solomon entered, taking his seat. The head of his guard, Abinadab, stood to their king's right.

"Abinadab, tell them what you told me earlier."

Abinadab bowed. "Yes, sir." He squared his shoulders, facing the crowd. "Earlier today, at the changing of the guard for the Ark of the Covenant, the previous shift was discovered missing. I was notified, and upon investigation, discovered blood on the floor. As it is forbidden to enter the chamber containing the holy relic, a rabbi was sent for, and he entered. The bodies of the guards were found inside, stabbed to death, and the Ark of the Covenant was gone."

Gasps erupted, shocked glances exchanged, Saul ignoring the terrified stares of those few fully aware of what had transpired the night before.

"Who would dare take it?" demanded someone from the crowd.

"And why hasn't God stricken them down?"

Solomon raised a hand, silencing them, then indicated to Abinadab to continue. "Search teams were immediately dispatched, and every dwelling and building will be searched. The city has been sealed, and no one may enter or leave without being searched. If it is here, we will find it."

"Surely they would have known that you'd search," said Michal, a young nobleman who had sacrificed nothing to Solomon's folly, his own firstborn a mere child. "It can only be an enemy of our people who would do such a thing, and if so, they would have taken it out of the city before we even discovered their blasphemous actions."

Nods of assent filled the room, Saul's head bobbing along with them, for Michal was right. His son and the others had taken it from the city immediately upon stealing it, and it was now part of the caravan returning to Menelik's kingdom, a full day's journey ahead, the sun now already setting on the city.

Solomon rose, silencing any speculation. "An enemy of our people is certainly responsible, however it is not an enemy from outside the walls of our great city, but from within."

"Surely not!" cried several, the howls of protest lost on Saul as beads of sweat clustered on his forehead and upper lip, his feet slowly carrying him backward, deeper into the crowd as Solomon's eyes scanned those gathered for him, he was certain.

"We have been betrayed, my friends, all of us." His voice cracked and lowered as he dropped back onto his throne. "But mostly I."

Saul halted his retreat, his eyes narrowing. Solomon's words were unexpected, and not those the man would have uttered if he knew who was truly involved.

"Who has betrayed us?" asked someone, the crowd hushed.

Solomon's shoulders sagged and his head drooped. "It can only be my son, Menelik."

Outrage tore through the room, and Saul sucked in a deep breath as his shaking body found the relief it so desperately needed. He could imagine no better outcome than this. No one in this room had liked Menelik. It wasn't because of who he was, but because of what his father had wanted for him. And now that Solomon believed his own son had betrayed him, had stolen their most precious possession, any chance of Menelik becoming Solomon's heir was gone.

And his own family's involvement would never be discovered.

Solomon wallowed in self-pity for several moments as the anger of those gathered continued to grow, demands for Menelik's head nearly unanimous. Saul caught the eye of the other fathers involved, all relieved, and they slowly gathered in a cluster of their own, saying nothing lest this glorious stroke of luck turn.

God is smiling on us today.

And He had to be. Clearly, they had done the right thing in liberating His gift to the Jewish people, and sending it with the best and brightest His chosen people had to offer. He was granting them His protection from any who might harm His children, with the knowledge that in time, when His children had fulfilled their task in this foreign land, they would return, with the Ark, to Jerusalem, so it could once again protect all His children from their enemies.

It filled his heart with joy to know he had done the right thing in God's eyes, and he faced Solomon with renewed vigor, confident in the decision he had made only a day ago.

Solomon raised a hand, his head still low, his eyes staring at his feet. The crowd grew silent, and the man spoke, his voice weak with grief. "I have dispatched riders to find the caravan, and inform the firstborn of Jerusalem of Menelik's treachery. It will be them who correct this injustice, and return not only the Ark to its rightful place, but the traitor as well." Solomon lifted his head, his bloodshot eyes staring out at his court. "I will kill him by my own hand."

Saul smiled as he inhaled deeply, this turning out even better than he could have imagined. All that was needed was for Solomon's messengers to reach the caravan, and his son would act. If all went well, they might be home before the sun set tomorrow.

God willing.

Milton Residence

St. Paul, Maryland

Present Day

"We're leaving on a quick trip tomorrow. Should be back in a week, I'm guessing."

Gregory Milton, Dean of St. Paul's University and James Acton's best friend, eyed him. "You're guessing?"

Acton shrugged. "Too vague?"

"What do you think?"

Milton's wife, Sandra, swatted her husband's shoulder. "Be nice, dear." She turned to her guests. "So, where are you two off to this time?"

Acton grinned. "Can't say!"

Milton threw up his hands. "You're impossible! You do know you work for me?"

Acton held up a finger. "Personal time. It's spring break."

"You're supposed to be at work on Monday."

Acton coughed, rubbing his throat. "I feel a cold coming on. Do you want a doctor's note?"

"Damned right I do!"

Acton turned to his wife. "Doctor, I need a note."

Laura Palmer grinned. "Sure thing, darlin'."

Milton rolled his eyes. "Not *that* kind of doctor."

Laura laughed. "Oh, Greg, you're just one big button that demands to be pushed."

Sandra ran her fingers through the hair on the back of her husband's head. "Hon, you *are* too easy to tease sometimes." She turned back to Laura. "You two *are* teasing, right?"

Acton shook his head. "I'm afraid not. We *are* leaving tomorrow, and should be back within a week, but we can't say where."

Milton regarded him. "Why?"

"We promised."

"Who?"

"The man who asked us to help him."

"But I'm your best friend."

"Which is exactly why I can't tell you anything."

Milton eyed him suspiciously as he leaned forward. "Is this something dangerous?"

Acton shrugged. "I hope not. Possibly."

Milton grabbed his beer, draining half the glass, then sat back, cradling it in his lap. "What is it with you two? I can understand when you're caught up in a dangerous situation, but why, when you *know* it is dangerous, do you still go charging in?"

Acton made a face. "I'm making sure my biographer has plenty to work with when I'm gone?"

Milton grunted. "They should make a movie of your lives."

Laura grinned. "A series of movies, like James Bond."

Sandra cooed. "Idris Elba could play Jim!"

Acton gave her a look. "Don't get me started."

Laura reached out for Sandra. "He's dreamy, isn't he?"

Sandra agreed a little too vigorously. "I'd like to be stranded on a mountain with him."

Laura snickered. "I'd rather be stranded in a hot tub."

Acton's jaw dropped. "I'm sitting right here!"

Laura waved a dismissive hand. "Shhh, the ladies are talking now."

Milton eyed his friend. "And if *we* talk like that, we're pigs."

Sandra patted his knee. "You are, darling."

Milton tried to regain the upper hand. "So, you're leaving tomorrow?"

Acton nodded. "The last of the equipment we need arrived a couple of hours ago."

"Equipment? Just what are you doing on this trip?"

Acton gave a toothy smile. "Can't say."

"My God, you'd think you were CIA." Milton paused, eying him for a moment. "You'd tell me if they recruited you, wouldn't you?"

Acton delivered his best Sean Connery impression. "I would. But then I'd have to kill you."

"I've got a bad feeling."

Sandra glanced over her shoulder at her husband as she removed her makeup. "You always have a bad feeling when it comes to them."

Milton lay down on the bed, face first, his back aching. "That's not true." He reached around and massaged his old gunshot wound that had temporarily paralyzed him, a paralysis that he had been told would be lifelong. Fortunately, the doctors had been wrong. "I only have a bad feeling when they leave the country."

"Good thing Laura's rich. There's no way they'd be able to get travel insurance anymore."

"I'm surprised they haven't been put on a no-fly list just to protect the innocent."

Sandra giggled. "Here, let me do that for you." She straddled him and took over, his wife having taken a course in therapeutic massage after he had been shot.

He groaned. "Oh, God, that's the spot!"

"It's always the spot."

"Is it?"

"Yup. Every time I reach it, you say the same thing." She pushed harder.

"Aaah, definitely the spot!" he moaned, his entire body turning to putty. "Every time he goes off galivanting somewhere, my back acts up."

"Well, they're leaving in the morning, so there's nothing you can really do about it. You'll just have to hope they're going to be okay."

He frowned. "I don't know. This time it's different. Usually, someone at least has an idea where they are. I don't know if they're going to Toledo or Timbuktu."

"Which is safer?"

"You'd think Toledo, but who knows these days."

"Well, wherever is safer, is likely where they're *not* going."

Milton grunted. "If I just knew where they were going, I'd feel better."

"Hack their computer and find out."

He chuckled. "Right, because it's that easy."

"For some people it is."

Milton paused then rolled over, his wife now straddling the good parts. "Smart *and* beautiful. Are we talking about Tommy Granger?"

She grinned then ground her hips into him. "I'm definitely not talking about him." She moaned. "You be Idris."

Milton's eyes shot wide. "Umm, be prepared to be underwhelmed then."

She ground again. "Shut up. You're James Bond, and I'm—"

"Michelle Yeoh!"

She stopped, staring down at him. "You didn't take long to think about that."

He grinned then flipped her over, pressing against her. "I think of myself as more of a Pierce Brosnan than an Idris Elba."

She reached over and turned off the light, plunging the room into darkness. "I don't care who you are, Mr. Bond, just put those Thunderballs to work."

He laughed, his shoulders shaking as he failed to control it. She grabbed his hips and pulled hard. He groaned, killing any laughter, and enjoyed the fantasy, silently praying neither of them called out the wrong name.

Two Days Outside Jerusalem

10ᵗʰ Century BC

"Someone approaches from the rear!"

Jonathan turned in his saddle, the long caravan continuing its slow journey toward the Red Sea and eventually Africa, where this bastard son of a king, Menelik, was from. He didn't care if he was the son of a king. He wasn't Jewish, despite his claims to the contrary. Yes, pagans were converted to Judaism all the time, and that was a good thing, and they were welcomed into their new community.

But not this Menelik. Jonathan had heard Menelik's mother had visited over twenty years ago and converted, then returned to her kingdom, where there were no Jews beyond some scholars sent with her. How could she possibly know what it was like to be one of God's chosen? And how could her son? They were Jews in name only, and couldn't possibly know the ways of his people.

And couldn't possibly rule the Israelites.

The notion was ludicrous, and he agreed with his father.

Solomon had to be stopped.

It would be Jonathan's duty, and that of the others, to make certain Menelik never returned. They had the Ark to protect them from their enemies, but the enemy in their midst would have to be dispatched by themselves. And though his father hadn't suggested it, he was already formulating a plan on how to accomplish the task.

For Menelik would never reach his home.

How, he did not know.

Yet.

But in time, he'd formulate a plan, inform the others, and they would execute it, leaving no witnesses. Then they'd return home, with a tale as to how Menelik had been killed by some unknown enemy on the mysterious continent.

But what of the Ark? How do we explain that?

He smiled.

Menelik stole it!

He reached the rear of the caravan to find a breathless messenger coming to a halt, challenged by a small contingent of firstborns. As the senior among them, Jonathan addressed the man.

"Identify yourself."

"I am Jesse, a messenger from the court of King Solomon."

Jonathan suppressed his excitement. Could Solomon have changed his mind? He doubted it. More likely, the theft had been discovered.

But why only a messenger? Why not an army?

"What is your message?"

"By order of the King, you are to arrest Menelik and return him to Jerusalem."

Jonathan's eyes shot wide. "Why?"

"He has stolen the Ark of the Covenant!"

The others, all now in the know, exchanged uncomfortable looks, too many of them glancing at the cart containing their precious possession, held near the back of the caravan to minimize the chances of Menelik's people discovering it.

"What is that?" asked Jesse, urging his horse toward the cart. "What is under that cloth?"

Jonathan blocked his path. "It is none of your concern."

Jesse stared at him. "But I come under the authority of the king. I am to find the Ark and secure it with your help."

"The Ark is secure, I assure you."

Jesse's eyes narrowed. "You act as if you already knew it was here." His jaw dropped as he realized what was going on. "Menelik didn't steal it, *you* did!"

Jonathan drew his sword and plunged it into Jesse's stomach, twisting the blade and scrambling the man's innards. He yanked the blade free and tossed it to one of the others, then reached forward, slapping a hand over the man's mouth, silencing his final cries lest they attract the attention of those farther down the caravan.

The life drained and the body still, Jonathan secured him to his horse then sent it out into the night. If the man was lucky, his steed would return him home for a proper funeral, with no one the wiser as to how he had met his end.

"Why did you kill him?" asked Zimri. "Surely that wasn't necessary."

"He discovered our secret."

"*Your* secret. Most of us had no part in this treachery."

Jonathan regarded Zimri. "Would you rather the Ark not be here?"

"I'd rather us not all be traitors to our people."

"So, you would happily follow this bastard child to his backward kingdom, and spend years from your family trying to teach these heathens to be civilized, without God's protection?"

Zimri glared at him, then finally sighed, his shoulders slumping. "No." He waved at the horse disappearing in the distance. "But now what do we do? We can go home! The king wants Menelik. He thinks *he* stole the Ark, not you. Our orders are no longer valid."

Another of the noble firstborn agreed. "We should leave now, with the Ark. We can be in Jerusalem within two days. We'll tell them that Menelik escaped, but we managed to rescue the Ark."

Jonathan considered the idea. "But Menelik knows the truth, and if we leave him alive, he may return to find out what happened to us. You saw the king, how enamored he was with Menelik. He might believe him, then we will be suspected." He eyed them all. "It would only take one of you to break under questioning, and I swear, if I go down for this, I will bring you all with me for not having immediately arrested me when you discovered what I had done."

Zimri shook his head. "Some friend you are."

Jonathan frowned. "I did this for all of us, to protect us so that we *didn't* die. Do you really think I want any of you to die to protect me? We need a better plan, one that will confirm what the king already suspects."

"I think we should just return home, and pray Solomon believes us."

Jonathan shook his head. "You're forgetting one thing."

"And what's that?"

"We just killed the messenger?"

"*You* killed the messenger. But how is that important?"

"If we return without the messenger, don't you think the king will wonder how we knew to come back?"

Zimri cursed. "So, we're stuck on this ridiculous journey because you couldn't control your blade."

Jonathan regarded his friend, someone he had thought intelligent to this point. "Do you honestly think the king sent only one messenger?"

Zimri stared at him blankly.

"We can expect that at least several were sent to find us, and this was but the first to arrive. And if you all would simply listen to me rather than question me, I'll tell you exactly what we need to do to ensure we're home with our families inside of two days."

Zimri bristled. "Very well. What do you have planned?"

Jonathan gestured toward the cart with the Ark. "First, we need to do something about that."

Aksum Emperor Yohannes IV Airport

Aksum, Ethiopia

Present Day

Acton stepped down from their chartered jet, a Boeing Business Jet Convertible, much larger than they were accustomed to, their cargo much heavier than normal.

But it was still air-conditioned.

He tugged at his shirt, the heat already oppressive. "Good thing it isn't summer."

Laura appeared unaffected after years of desert digs. "On our way back, I want to stop at the dig in Egypt, see how my old students are doing."

Acton watched as the Ethiopian groundcrew quickly unloaded several pallets of equipment, along with supplies to tend to their needs should their hosts not be able to provide the basic necessities without sacrificing to the point it affected their own.

"You are true to your word!"

Acton turned to see a smiling Father Amanuel, his hands outstretched. He grasped Laura's shoulders, delivering a kiss to each cheek, then did the same to Acton.

"You have everything you need?"

Laura smiled. "Assuming the diesel generator arrived."

Amanuel nodded. "It arrived earlier. We've already loaded it."

"Excellent. It's of sufficient power to keep everything going, and we've brought a battery backup that will last several hours should there be any delays in refueling. We also have all the supplies necessary to build the portable containment chamber you requested."

Amanuel's head bobbed in appreciation as he eyed the pallets. Some words were exchanged, and soon everything was loaded into the back of several old trucks that appeared to be vintage World War Two surplus. "I am excited to get started on this project." He led them to a nearby notorious British luxury car that had seen better days, a Mercedes hood ornament replacing the jungle cat.

Does that make it more reliable?

"How far is it?"

"Not far." He held open the rear door. "You'll ride with me. It will be much more comfortable than the trucks."

Acton climbed in, sliding to the far side, and Laura followed. Amanuel joined them and closed the door. The driver, dressed in the yellow robes of a monk, started the car, and they pulled away, the trucks following. They drove in silence for some time, giving Acton an opportunity to take in the small, bustling city of Aksum. Long the poster child of poverty and failure, Ethiopia was slowly making a turnaround, and evidence of that surrounded them in the forms of new construction, and luxury goods hawked from street vendors and storefronts alike.

But the poverty was evident, too many emaciated frames peppering the street corners with hands out, begging for scraps or change. It made him thankful they had brought their own supplies, for he didn't expect there to be much to go around where they were heading.

This was among the poorest of the poor countries.

Yet cellphones abounded.

And weapons.

AK-47s and other variants seemed almost ubiquitous, and it had Acton wishing they had weapons of their own. He spotted an AK-47 on the front seat of their "Mercedes," and wondered if the driver knew how to use it, or if it was there for show.

A warrior monk?

It wasn't unheard of in history, the Templars the most obvious example, though he doubted he would be willing to put his life, or that of Laura's, into their driver's hands.

They soon left the city, Father Amanuel evidently more comfortable outside of the hustle and bustle of Aksum, now more animated in his hosting duties, pointing out various landmarks, churches, and places where he had preached in his younger days.

It was an interesting if bleak drive, and Acton found himself drifting in and out of sleep from the jetlag, when the driver made a sudden turn off the road and into the grass lining it, forcing Acton wide awake from the jolt of adrenaline surging through his body. He stared ahead, spotting

84

a slight trail carved through the grass, and said nothing, though Laura's hand was gripping his a little tighter than a moment before.

They came to a jarring stop, their driver using the emergency brake, making Acton wonder if they had any functioning regular brakes.

"We're here."

Acton squinted as he stared out the window. There was nothing in sight beyond a windswept plain, grass gently blowing in the breeze, a few scattered trees about.

And not a single structure that might house a person, let alone the Ark of the Covenant.

The driver opened the door for Father Amanuel, and Acton opened his own, stepping outside and making a quick scan of the area, still finding nothing, before helping Laura out.

He turned to Amanuel. "Where are we?"

"My church and my home."

Acton exchanged a confused look with Laura. "But there's nothing here."

"Looks can be deceiving."

Amanuel strode forward, toward nothing, as far as Acton was concerned, their transport trucks arriving and parking behind them. Acton took Laura's hand and they followed the elderly priest, Acton's head on a pivot as he tried to find any evidence of civilization when Laura tugged on his hand.

"Look!"

Acton turned and squinted at where she was pointing, not sure of what he was seeing. It appeared to be a moat, carved into the ground, a near-perfect rectangle, guarding another lying within. And as they neared, the first few steps of a staircase, cut into the bedrock, descending into the moat, became visible.

And he gasped as he realized what lay before them.

"Unbelievable!"

Approaching Elath

10th Century BC

Jonathan eyed the port ahead, one of Menelik's men already informing them that the boats had been arranged to take them through the gulf and into the Red Sea, then finally its western bank.

Yet they were never to have boarded the boats.

The expected messenger from King Solomon had never arrived. He had no explanation. They had to know their route, and would know this was one of their stops along it. He could only hope that a messenger was waiting for them in the city ahead, but if they were, it could prove problematic.

The caravan was long, and his carefully laid plan had assumed the messenger would approach from the rear. His men had moved the cart with the Ark farther along the caravan, mixing in with the tail end of Menelik's entourage. Their orders were to rejoin him and the others should a messenger arrive, so that when they searched the caravan for the Ark, it would be found among Menelik's men, with the messenger never having a chance to see it was guarded by the firstborns.

But if the messenger approached from the front, he would travel the length of the caravan looking for the firstborns, and the first he would encounter would be those guarding the Ark.

It would mean the complete failure of his plan, and this time killing the poor soul wouldn't be an option, as Menelik would see the man.

The entire situation had his heart pounding as they entered the valley leading to the port ahead, the glistening waters normally a beacon to those who approached, but for him, it was a constant reminder of impending doom.

For once they boarded the boats, no messenger would ever reach them, and he and the others would be doomed to spend the prime of their lives serving this bastard child.

Though there was another possibility.

His own friends might turn on him. He had heard grumblings, several already vocally blaming him for their situation, yet he had to remind them, firmly, that if he hadn't stolen the Ark, then no messenger would have ever been sent. It was his actions that had given them the only hope they had to escape their fate.

Though if his plan failed, and they were faced with no other option but to board the boats and leave their homeland behind, his friends might turn regardless.

"Raiders!"

He turned in his saddle, then redirected his gaze to where Zimri was pointing. He cursed. Two dozen riders lined the top of the ridge. He checked over his shoulder and cursed again, another two dozen on the opposite.

It was an ambush, and though the caravan had superior numbers, it was drawn out in a long line. By the time Menelik's men could reach them to help, many of his brothers would be dead.

"What's going on?"

Jonathan turned to see David and the others guarding the Ark arrive. "What are you doing here?"

"We heard shouting," replied David. "I thought it was the signal."

Jonathan shook his head, drawing his sword then pointing it at the raiders now cresting the ridge and rushing toward them. "We're about to be attacked, you fools!"

A roar went up and his men split into two ranks, one each to face the bandits. Arrows from several of those skilled in archery were loosed, but they were few, most firstborn of Jerusalem preferring the sword to the less honorable bow.

"The cowards are running!" yelled David.

Jonathan readied himself for the onslaught, no intent to retreat evident, and glanced behind him to find the same. But as his eyes returned to the enemy he faced, he spotted what David had.

Menelik's men were abandoning them, racing for the ships.

And to his horror, taking the cart containing the Ark with them.

"We have to stop them!"

But it was too late.

He swung his blade, catching his opponent in the chest and knocking him from his saddle, then pushed forward, realizing there was little he could do now. He made eye contact with the next of his enemy and shifted in his saddle as his horse, well trained and experienced in battle, snorted in anticipation.

His opponent swung and Jonathan parried the blow, leaning back in his saddle as the deflected blade slid up his own and over his head harmlessly. He righted himself, turning to reengage when Zimri finished the man off before he had a chance to regain his balance.

"They're trying to cut us off!"

He checked to his right and cursed at the sight, the caravan now in the distance, inside the city, the gentle slope that led to the port giving him an unfettered view of Menelik's men rushing their leader to the safety of the sea.

Though tempted to condemn them for their cowardice, they were merely doing their job. If the roles were reversed, and it was King Solomon that he was protecting, he too would leave Menelik's men behind to deal with the threat while leading his liege to safety.

Yet the roles weren't reversed.

It was he and his friends left to die.

"Regroup! Archers to the center!" he ordered, the half-dozen masters of the bow falling back behind the rows of cavalry, shielded from the enemies' swords. "Target the left flank! Pick your targets!"

Arrows flew as his men closed ranks, the heft of their steeds, pressed together, creating an impenetrable wall against the raiders, all reduced to battling by sword except the archers, who quickly thinned the enemy on their left flank.

To the point they broke ranks and turned tail, rushing back up the ridge from whence they had come. Jonathan smiled, turning to face those who would keep them from the sea and the Ark. "Archers, target the right flank!" He motioned for those defending the now abandoned left flank to follow him. "To the sea!"

They charged forward, penetrating the dwindling numbers they faced, Jonathan delivering one last fatal blow before breaking through and racing toward the port ahead. He could see the boats being prepared, Menelik's men quickly loading their cargo with the help of workers no doubt generously rewarded by the wealthy man.

"Retreat!" shouted someone behind him, and he stood in his saddle, staring back to see what was happening, and gasped in horror. Dozens more were now on the ridges, pouring into the battle, the remaining firstborns now racing after him.

He had split their forces, a mistake his enemy had no doubt counted on.

You fool!

Yet he had no choice. He couldn't let the Ark leave without him. It would be an unforgivable sin. But his decision had left the others weakened and vulnerable, all their provisions and cargo, including gifts for the queen, Menelik's mother, now vulnerable.

Things can be replaced. The best and brightest of Jerusalem can't.

He waved for them to follow, his own voice joining the call to retreat, those left behind abandoning the fight and rushing to join the others, leaving the heavily laden carts behind.

A small price to pay for his friends' lives, though he wondered if Solomon would feel the same way.

The bandits immediately set upon their bounty, forgetting those they had just engaged, their purpose not to kill, but to loot caravans foolish enough to fall into their trap.

Yet it was a bold move. The caravan had been large in numbers, though the wealth on display must have been too tempting a target.

Thank God Menelik's men took the Ark with them, even if it was unknowingly.

He stared ahead and cried out at the sight before him. The first of the boats was already departing, no doubt with Menelik aboard, its sail full, God blessing them with a good wind, the oars in the water barely needed.

"Hurry! We can't let them leave!"

They charged through the city gates and through the streets busy with merchants and travelers, their way blocked on too many occasions as more boats departed. As they finally approached the harbor, his brothers left behind now safely inside the city, the raiders unlikely to pursue them, he stood in his saddle, waving at the departing boats, the last of Menelik's men pulling from the dock.

"Stop!" he cried, collapsing in his saddle as he spotted the cart he and his father had used to steal the Ark, now empty, its covered cargo nowhere to be seen.

What have I done?

He spotted Menelik at the stern of the lead boat, waving to them. "Take the boats, follow us!"

"You must wait! You have the Ark!"

Menelik shook his head, pressing a cupped hand to his ear. "What?"

"You have the Ark of the Covenant!"

But it was no use. The man couldn't hear him, and even if he did, what could he expect of him? There was no turning back, as the risk was too great, and what possible incentive would he have to wait for them?

Their choice was clear, and it was unfortunately the only one left to them.

"To the boats!" he ordered, the firstborns rushing onto the remaining boats, their horses loaded onto the decks as the sails were unfurled, the oars manned.

Yet there was no wind. He turned, staring after Menelik's boats, their sails full, the distance rapidly growing between them as the others rowed as hard as they could, none trained for the task, the crews provided by the boats' owners merely there to man the tiller and navigate.

Please God, give us the wind like you did Menelik!

But the sails remained empty as the boats containing the most important possession of the Jewish people disappeared on the horizon, God already delivering His judgment, and finding him and the others unworthy of His help.

Forgive me for what I have done.

He stared up at the heavens, dropping to his knees as he clasped his hands in front of him, tears streaking his cheeks.

"Please, God, punish me for what I have done, but do not punish my people! They still require your protection!"

The response was deafening in its silence. The sails remained empty, and Menelik was out of sight, with the future of the Jewish people unknowingly in his possession.

Never again to see the lands of his people.

Granger/Trinh Residence

St. Paul, Maryland

Present Day

Gregory Milton knocked on the door of the apartment, checking the number again. He had never been here before, visiting students at their homes not exactly encouraged by Human Resources.

But this was different.

He had asked Tommy Granger to commit a crime.

A small one.

Though still something that could throw them all in jail.

Yet he had no choice. He had to know where his friend was, and Tommy was the only person he knew who could find out quickly and easily. The kid was a genius on the computer, could hack pretty much any system out there, and had been arrested in his youth for doing just that—he had hacked the Department of Defense.

The door opened and Tommy's girlfriend, and one of Acton's grad students, Mai Trinh, smiled at him. "Dean Milton. Please, come in."

She moved aside and he stepped in, removing his shoes before following her deeper inside. Tommy was at his laptop and gave him a wave. "Hiya, sir. Just in time."

Milton advanced, forgetting his earlier misgivings. "You found out where they went?"

"You could say that. And I don't think you're going to like it."

Milton's heart rate picked up a few beats. "Why? Where are they?"

"Their cellphones are inactive now, but the last towers they pinged off of were in some place called Aksum."

"Ethiopia!"

Tommy smiled at him. "Say, you're good. Mai had to tell me where that was."

Milton dropped into a chair, shaking his head. "Ethiopia! Why the hell would they go there?"

Tommy shrugged. "You got me. Want me to hack their accounts? Maybe there's something there."

Milton was tempted, but shook his head. "No, that would be violating their privacy." He sighed. "Why couldn't it have been Berlin or Paris? Then I wouldn't be worrying." He stared at Tommy's laptop, a set of phone numbers listed.

"What's that?"

"Just their latest calls. Do you want me to print them out for you?"

Milton shook his head. "No, let's try to respect what remains of their privacy." He pursed his lips, thinking for a moment as he tried to figure out where the fine line of legitimate concern and invasion of privacy sat. "Umm, can you set up something on the Internet to monitor for any news coming out of Ethiopia? You know, anything that might suggest the shit's hit the fan with them again?"

Tommy cracked his knuckles with a flourish. "That's my jam."

"Uh huh."

"Do you want me to monitor the Dark Web too?"

"You mean that underground Internet thing?"

"Yes."

Milton nodded. "Do whatever's legal."

Tommy eyed him. "Why? We just broke the law checking their phones."

Milton groaned then waved his hands in front of him. "I don't want to know anything else. Forget I asked."

"Copy that."

He said his goodbyes, but before Mai could close the door behind him, he heard Tommy's fingers attacking the keyboard.

And smiled.

Good boy.

Acton/Palmer Residence

St. Paul, Maryland

Dawit Ganno held his breath as their New York City operative, Asrat Fida, expertly disabled the security alarm in the professors' residence.

"You're sure nobody was notified?"

"Positive. It gives you enough time to enter your code and I was able to disable it before that."

"So, you have been making good use of your time here."

Fida frowned. "There's not much else to do."

Ganno detected a hint of snark. "Remember, you're here doing God's work."

Fida said nothing, instead heading deeper into the house. "How about we get this over with. I may have stopped the security company from knowing we're here, but that doesn't mean a neighbor didn't see us."

Ganno grunted, Fida's point correct. "What are we looking for? I'm not used to an American household."

"Anything electronic, or any papers. iPhones, iPads, tablets, eReaders, laptops, desktops—"

"You realize most of those words mean nothing to me."

Fida nodded. "You look for papers, I'll look for devices."

"Very well."

The search didn't take long, Fida returning to the living area within minutes, emptyhanded. "They must have taken everything with them."

Ganno eyed him skeptically. "Who takes a computer with them? Aren't they kind of bulky?"

Fida chuckled. "You really are in the Dark Ages, aren't you? They probably have laptops. Portable computers. You just disconnect it and put it in a bag."

"Ahh, yes, I've seen those before. I didn't realize they were as useful as a computer."

"They are now." Fida gestured at the home in general. "There's nothing here to check."

"What about their email, I think you call it? Can you get into that? Isn't that stored on the Internet?"

"Sometimes, but we'd need to know their email addresses, and depending on how secure they are, we could just trigger an alert." Fida shook his head. "I think it's best we leave well enough alone."

"We need to know if they told anyone."

Fida shrugged. "We listened in with the parabolic on their dinner with their friends last night, and they said nothing. I think they're going to keep their promise to Father Amanuel."

"They better. I really don't want to have to kill anyone but them." He pointed at a pile of papers sitting on the kitchen counter. "I found these. Take a look. I can't read English very well."

Fida stepped over and quickly leafed through the pages, his eyes widening. "These look like they're for the equipment they referred to." His eyes narrowed as he continued to examine them, taking photos of each with his phone. "It looks like it's equipment for some sort of containment system." He looked at Ganno. "Is there something wrong with the Ark?"

"What do you mean?"

"Well, judging by these papers and these measurements, it looks like they've been asked by Father Amanuel to build something to help protect the Ark."

"Protect it how?"

"It looks like this system would control the temperature and humidity."

Ganno's jaw dropped slightly. "So, that's why he left. I've been trying to figure out why the Keeper would leave that which he has sworn to protect with his life. But if something had happened to it, or was going to happen to it, then protecting it might mean seeking help."

Fida pursed his lips then exhaled. "So, we don't have to worry about them."

Ganno shook his head. "On the contrary. It merely changes the timing."

"What do you mean?"

"Now we wait until they finish their job."

100

"But they're good people, doing a good thing."

"It doesn't matter. They know the secret, and that can't be allowed to stand."

"But do they? For all we know, Father Amanuel didn't tell them what it was. They might be just going to show him how everything works, then leave, never knowing what they're preserving."

Ganno's head bobbed slowly as he scratched his nose. "This is possible, but we would need to be sure. If the professors enter the church, then they must die."

Leroux/White Residence, Fairfax Towers
Falls Church, Virginia

"That's why I'm glad I can't have any social media accounts."

CIA Analyst Supervisor Chris Leroux rolled over and faced his girlfriend, CIA Agent Sherrie White. "Why? You don't trust yourself?"

She grinned. "With my propensity for calling out stupid? I'd be unemployable, at least within the government."

Leroux laughed, his eyes drooping from the post-coital bliss he was still enjoying. Sherrie had just returned from a mission, and whenever she did, she was wired and horny. A potent combination that he always enjoyed the benefits of, especially when he didn't need to be at work in a few hours.

And today he didn't.

They had all day to enjoy the treasures each had to offer, though he was certain he was getting the better end of the bargain.

"Yeah, you might be right. That's why I shut mine all down. That and the fact I had almost no friends, so it was just depressing."

Sherrie gave him a quick peck. "If I were allowed, I would have been your friend."

"You and my mom. Yay!"

She laughed. "I've read some of the stuff your Mom posts. She's the type us Millennials would dox if she were found out."

"She just tells her friends what she thinks about things. Unfortunately, she doesn't understand privacy settings."

"It's ridiculous, though, right? You've got people destroying careers and lives because of things they did ten, twenty, thirty years ago. These same people demand that people change, then claim that because somebody said something thirty years ago that was racist or homophobic, they must still be racist or homophobic. They never consider that the person, like most of society, has changed. Instead, they're out for blood." She sighed. "My poor boy, Liam. Sexiest old dude I know getting raked over the coals for something that happened forty years ago."

Leroux grunted. "How did I know this was all about him?"

"He's my boy, you know it."

"I think you have daddy issues."

She gave him a toothy smile. "Who's your daddy? You want to ask me it, don't you?"

"Well, not now."

She put a leg behind her head. "Now?"

His eyes bulged. "Umm…"

The acrobatics ended. "What comes around goes around though."

"It does tend to do that."

"I hope some of these trolls that are demanding vengeance for things said decades ago get their comeuppance eventually. Someday, there will be something considered politically incorrect that they make fun of today, and I just hope they get their lives destroyed for it."

"That's pretty harsh. Like what? It's pretty much taboo to make fun of anybody for anything now."

She shook her head. "You can't make fun of anyone for their race, color, creed, religion, sexual orientation, whether they're too tall or too short or handicapped in some way. But there's one thing you can still make fun of, with impunity, that I think will change eventually, and there will be millions of these hypocrites with examples of it literally peppering their Instagram accounts and Facebook pages."

Leroux racked his brain, trying to think of what she could possibly be referring to. "I give up. What?"

"Fat people, especially men. TV shows, movies, memes, everything, are still making fun of fat people, just like twenty years ago when they were making fun of homosexuals."

Leroux had to agree. Weight was never his problem, nor did he think it ever was Sherrie's, but he had noticed over the years they had known each other, she rarely laughed at anything that made fun of obese people. "You're right, of course, they are the only people it's still open season on." Her face clouded over and he took her hand. "Tell me."

Her eyes filled with tears and he held her close.

"What is it? What's wrong?"

"It was my dad."

"What, he was overweight?"

"Yes. He was always struggling, always battling it, trying everything, but he could never lose it, not permanently. I remember him always trying so hard, and always failing, before he finally gave up. He said it wasn't worth making himself miserable over, and if it killed him, then so be it." She gasped, quickly sucking the breath back in. "I remember...I remember, just before he was killed, that he said he'd rather die young and happy, than old and miserable." Her shoulders shook. "The worst part of it, though, was that I knew he was miserable. He was a prisoner in his own body. He was always so full of life when I was young, even though he was overweight, but when he went on Insulin and gained so much more, it killed him inside. He was never the same."

He held her tight, this a rare occasion, Sherrie almost never talking about her parents, both having been killed in a car accident when she was a teenager. "It's okay. He's in a better place now."

"I-I hope so. At least his suffering is over." Her shoulders shook. "I just miss them so much."

He ran his hand over the back of her head as she gently cried, her breathing slowly becoming regular before she fell asleep in his arms. He found his own tears flowing now, never having seen the woman he loved so affected by anything so personal. He felt closer to her now, now that he had seen her so vulnerable for the first time, and wanted to protect her from all the hate in the world, despite the fact she was the one who protected him.

His phone vibrated on the nightstand and he extricated himself as gently as he could, his efforts futile as she woke up.

"Sorry, did I fall asleep?"

"Like a baby." He grabbed his phone, holding it up. "It's Sonya."

"Ahh, the other woman in your life."

He grinned at the reference to his underling's crush on him. "I *am* a popular guy." He swiped his thumb. "Hi, Sonya, what's up?"

"Hello, sir, sorry to bother you on your day off, but I thought you should know that Professor Acton's house was just broken into."

Leroux propped himself up against the headboard. He had dealt with Acton and his wife on far too many occasions, their knack for getting into trouble legendary at Langley and Fort Bragg. "Have the police been notified?"

"No, this was an expert job. The system was deactivated before it had a chance to go off."

"Then how do we know about it?"

"Special Agent Kane had a backup installed when we were dealing with the Assembly threat. It was never taken out, and the thieves didn't know to bypass it."

"Where are the professors now?"

"Ethiopia."

"What the hell are they doing there?"

"No idea."

Leroux sighed. "Okay, check the cameras in the neighborhood, see if they caught anything. I'm going to talk to Dylan, see if he wants to do anything, since this was his ask."

"Okay, I'll let you know what we find."

Leroux ended the call and turned to Sherrie, now sitting cross-legged beside him, any trace of her earlier emotional outburst gone. "So, what have the professors got themselves into this time?"

Leroux chewed his cheek for a moment. "Not sure. Their house was broken into. Professional job. A backup Dylan had installed got tripped, so that's the only reason we know about it."

Sherrie bounced closer, a bit of impressive yogic flying executed. "I'm off for two days. I could go check it out." She brightened. "I could take Fang! I know she'd kill to do something with a little bit of excitement."

Leroux smiled at her enthusiasm. "Sounds good to me. Just remember, if you're caught, you're on your own."

She executed the perfect pout. "You'll break up with me?"

He extended his hand. "Hi, Chris Leroux, nerd loser who knows nothing about women. Nice to meet you."

She slapped his hand away. "You know I hate it when you put yourself down." She reached over and squeezed Chris Jr. "And you definitely know a thing or two about women." She winked. "Or at least he does."

Kane/Fang Residence, Fairfax Towers
Falls Church, Virginia

CIA Special Agent Dylan Kane pushed as hard as he could, the treadmill reaching its limit as his heart threatened to explode. His body dripped with sweat, his veins bulged, and to his astonishment, he still couldn't match his girlfriend's speed.

And he finally gave up trying, reaching forward and reducing the speed by a few notches, the reprieve welcomed by his struggling heart as Lee Fang, former Chinese Special Forces, and now exile in hiding, continued her blistering pace.

"You're a machine."

She grinned. "When you have nothing else to do, you have plenty of time to work on your cardio." Her iPhone beeped, her sixty minutes up, and she eased off, beginning her cooldown. "Want to go for a run after this?"

Kane's eyes bulged as he slowed to an easy jog. "Are you nuts?"

She giggled. "Or we could hit the shower. Together."

Kane's eyebrows bounced suggestively. "Now, I like the sound of that." He yanked the safety clip from the treadmill, killing the unit. "Race you?"

"You'd lose."

The doorbell rang and Kane cursed. "I bet that's Chris. Ever since we moved into his building, he seems to be hellbent on revenge for all those times I interrupted him and Sherrie from bumpin' uglies."

He folded up his treadmill as Fang did the same, pushing them both into the closet before grabbing a towel.

The doorbell rang again.

"I'm coming! I'm coming!" He jogged over to the door and peeked through the peephole, smiling with satisfaction. "Told you!" He opened the door and greeted his best friend and his other half. "Hey, guys, come on in." He stepped aside and grinned at Leroux's flushed face and awkward smile. "Hey, you got some, didn't you?"

Leroux went full red.

"Twice!" confirmed Sherrie.

"My man!" Kane offered up a fist bump which Leroux reluctantly tapped. Fang walked over, a housecoat wrapped around her lithe frame, and handed Kane a bottle of water, her own well underway.

"So, to what do we owe the pleasure? I thought we were having dinner tomorrow night." Fang's eyes widened. "Oh no, did I get the dates wrong?"

Sherrie shook her head. "No, no, this is all business."

Fang brightened. "Ooh, I like business!"

Kane gave her a quick squeeze around the shoulders. "My babe does love shooting at things." He led their guests into the living room and was about to sit when Fang swatted him.

"Don't you dare sit that sweaty bum on my couch."

Kane hovered, his ass inches from the seat, then stood, Fang tossing him a dry towel to sit on. He spread it out then sat. "Happy?"

"Elated."

"Good." He returned his attention to Leroux. "So, what's going on?"

"I got a call from Sonya."

Kane grinned. "During?"

Sherrie cocked her head. "Would that technically be a threesome if the person on the other end of the line wants to do the slap and tickle with the other person?"

Leroux shook his head, closing his eyes. "Who would have ever thought *I'd* be the one with women troubles."

"Buddy, it's a lucky man who has two women that want him. And it's a stupid man that acts on it."

Sherrie patted Leroux's cheek. "I trust my man."

Leroux rolled his eyes. "I hate being lucky." He held up a hand, cutting off Sherrie's no doubt witty response. "Anyway, Sonya said that Professor Acton's house was just broken into. Professional job. They bypassed the alarm, but didn't know about the backup you had installed when we were dealing with the Assembly."

Kane leaned back, concerned. Professor Acton was his former archaeology professor at university, before he dropped out to join the Army and fight terrorism. It had been Acton that acted as his advisor

110

during the difficult decision. "I forgot I had done that." Kane paused. "You don't think it's the Assembly, do you?"

Leroux shook his head. "We haven't heard from them since we took them down. No, this is something else."

Kane nodded. "We should check it out."

Sherrie agreed. "That's what we were thinking. I'll go, and Fang, if you want to come—"

Fang was hopping up and down in excitement. "Yes, please!"

Kane smiled at the love of his life, a woman he had rescued from the Chinese government after she had technically committed treason to stop rogue generals from conspiring in a coup attempt in the United States. Their shared loneliness had drawn them together, and outside of his official duties, they were now inseparable.

And he loved to see her excited.

"If you two do this, Fang does all the dirty work."

Sherrie's lower lip shoved out. "Awww!"

Leroux chuckled. "No, he's right. You have to stay in the car and provide backup. We can't have a CIA agent breaking into a private residence." He paused, his eyes taking on that distant stare they all knew so well. It meant Kane's friend was about to have an epiphany.

"Uh oh. Some knowledge is about to drop," warned Kane.

Sherrie snickered. "I love it when he does that."

Leroux snapped back to reality. "I was thinking—"

Kane gave him a look. "No, really?"

His friend flipped him the bird. "I was thinking, maybe we're going about this all wrong."

"What do you mean?" asked Fang.

"Well, you guys are all spies, so you always think of getting into a place without anyone knowing."

Sherrie turned to face him on the loveseat. "What are you getting at?"

"Well, why not just go in with permission?"

Fang frowned. "Where's the fun in that?"

Kane patted her leg. "What do you mean?"

"I mean, surely his best friend, Greg Milton, has a spare key. Just tell him what's going on, he'll let you in, and nobody is breaking any laws."

Fang's frown turned into a pout. "You're no fun."

Leroux shrugged. "Maybe, but this way you all survive the day without criminal records."

Kane sighed. "Sorry, dear, but he's right."

Fang folded her arms. "He may be, but he's still no fun."

Unknown Location

South of Aksum, Ethiopia

Acton's heart pounded with excitement. He had seen these churches before, though only in pictures, and those did the actual structure little justice. These rock-cut monolithic churches were carved directly into the bedrock, down into the earth. It left a flat surface to the naked eye from a distance, but at the edge of the outside cuts, a full structure was visible in the center, including windows and doorways.

It was breathtaking work, performed centuries ago, providing not only security from a distance, but a reprieve from the desert heat.

"I've always dreamed of seeing one of these," murmured Laura, in awe as he was.

Father Amanuel smiled. "I guess I sometimes forget how unique these are to outsiders. I've lived in and among them most of my life, so I guess I've grown accustomed to them." He beckoned them to follow him down the stairs carved into the earth on one of the four sides, leading them to the bottom of the excavation, then through a doorway made from wood, a cross etched over its arch. They entered an outer chamber, another set of doors ahead of them.

Laura gripped Acton's hand and squeezed. He returned it as he trembled with excitement.

"Are we about to see what I think we're about to see?"

Amanuel smiled. "Yes. You are about to see what few have in thousands of years, ever since King Menelik ordered it hidden from his people." The elderly priest removed a key from around his neck, and unlocked the second set of doors. He stepped inside and Acton followed Laura after him, the natural light from windows carved above gone, only torchlight now lighting their way.

Gleaming off the copious amounts of gold cladding the vessel built thousands of years ago, to the exacting specifications provided by God.

Shivers rushed over his body like waves as he took in the sight, the two cherubim, their wings arched forward as they bowed toward the mercy seat meant for communion with God Himself, had his chest aching at their beauty, the artisans responsible demonstrating their faith and respect through their God-given skills.

"It's beautiful," he whispered, almost afraid to speak in its presence.

Laura stepped closer, her hand extending to touch it, when he finally realized what she was doing.

"No!" He surged forward, grabbing her and pulling her back. "Don't touch it, remember? Only by the poles."

She gave him a look. "You don't believe that, do you?"

"Are you willing to take that chance?"

She frowned, but shoved her hands into her pockets. "Perhaps it's better to be safe than sorry." She circled the Ark, examining it carefully, Acton doing the same in the opposite direction. He reached out and ran his hand along the poles used to carry the Ark, the only part of the creation allowed to be touched by man.

And frowned.

"This is a fake!" he cried.

Laura rushed around to see what he had found. "What is it?"

He pointed at the pole. "Look at the wood. What would you say that is?"

She leaned in, shaking her head. "I'm not sure, but it's definitely not acacia." She turned to Amanuel, who remained by the door. "Why would you waste our time like this?"

Acton stared at the elderly priest with a combination of disappointment and rage. "And all that money? What possible reason could you have?"

Amanuel held up his hands in defense. "I'm sorry, I didn't know." He stepped closer, eying the Ark. "I'm sure you're mistaken."

Acton shook his head vehemently. "I'm not." He eyed Amanuel. "And you know it. You're intentionally showing us a fake, aren't you?"

Amanuel stood, saying nothing, before finally sighing. "It's forbidden for anyone outside our order to see the real Ark. If word of its existence were to get out, so many would flock to it, that it would be lost for sure."

"But isn't it lost already?" Laura ran her hand along the fake. "Nobody has seen it for so long, it might as well be."

Amanuel shook his head. "No, it is merely forgotten. By design."

115

Acton's eyes narrowed. "By design?"

"Yes. At first, King Menelik ordered the Ark hidden so it couldn't be abused by his grandson, who wanted to use it to conquer the kingdom's enemies. Jewish rabbis were given the honor of fulfilling Menelik's directive, his instructions to keep the Ark hidden forever followed for a millennium. When our Lord Jesus Christ was born, and we converted to Christianity, things changed. He spoke of a time when the Ark would be forgotten, because it would no longer be needed to commune with God, because all man would be united under Him in Jerusalem."

Acton bit his lip for a moment. "So, your interpretation is that this unity He spoke of can never come to pass as long as mankind knows of the Ark."

Amanuel nodded. "Good. You understand. If word were to get out and the actual Ark were to be seen by the public, there would be a renewed reverence for it, and while it may rally many of mankind to its altar, it would mean the prophecy could never come true. Mankind would never unite under Jesus, because mankind would never have forgotten about the Ark."

Laura, always the pragmatist, spoke first. "If you don't want mankind to see it, and you actually want them to forget it even exists, then why not let it crumble? Why bring us here to preserve it?"

"Because it is the Ark. Nothing was ever said about destroying it, or letting it turn to dust. Our duty is to hide it until the prophecy is fulfilled."

Acton scratched his neck. "Why not give it to the Vatican? Surely they could protect it."

Amanuel grunted. "They would put it on display, for all to see, forever. The prophecy would be doomed for certain."

Acton frowned. "But you've been telling everyone you've had it for decades, if not centuries."

Amanuel smiled. "And did you believe us?"

"Well, no, I guess not."

"Exactly. There are dozens of churches here that claim to have the Ark, many with replicas just like this. All swear theirs is real, and since they all can't be, everyone assumes none are."

"Yet you want us to believe yours is."

Amanuel held up his hands and shrugged. "You must have faith, my son."

Laura exhaled loudly. "Well, Father, if we're to show you how to preserve the *real* Ark, we'll need to see it."

Amanuel shook his head. "Absolutely not. Just show us how on this replica, and we'll do the rest."

Laura waved a hand, cutting off any discussion. "No. We need to see what the actual damage is before we can know for certain how to preserve it. We have to adjust the equipment to maintain the correct conditions for its current state." She shook her head. "No, if you want our help, we have to see the real thing, otherwise just take us back to the airport now. You can keep the equipment, but I warn you, if you don't set it up correctly, you could do more harm than good."

Amanuel regarded her for some time before he finally sighed, his shoulders sagging in defeat. "Very well. But there is an old saying, Professor." He shouted something in what Acton assumed was Amharic, and four men entered the room, AK-47s held to their chests. "Be careful

what you wish for."

Upper Egypt

10ᵗʰ Century BC

Menelik stood on the shore of the Red Sea, staring at the horizon as he shielded his eyes, the firstborn sons of Jerusalem nowhere to be found. It was curious, what had happened, and he had no explanation for it. The sails of all his ships were full, the oars barely used the entire journey, yet the wind had failed the others.

Why?

Travel by sea was a novelty for him, but the captains of the vessels they had hired seemed as perplexed as he was.

Yet that wasn't what concerned him the most. It was what one of them had shouted, something he must have heard incorrectly.

You have the Ark of the Covenant.

He must have misheard the man, yet he was certain enough that he hadn't, to order the boats to unload on an abandoned stretch of coastline rather than the port, where they might be searched by Egyptian authorities.

For if they did indeed have the Ark of the Covenant in their possession, and someone were to discover that fact, those who would desire it would stop at nothing to possess it.

Including killing all his men.

Even he found his own heart pounding at the excitement as the vessels were unloaded. He knew the fathers of the firstborn had requested the Ark be sent with their children, but Solomon had denied it. There was no way his father had changed his mind, which must mean they had stolen it then hidden it among the supplies and gifts sent by Solomon for his mother.

Surely Father must know by now.

Yet if that were the case, wouldn't he have sent men to recover it? Why had no one come to tell him that thieves were in his midst with the most precious of bounties? It made no sense.

His eyes narrowed as he continued to piece together the mystery he faced. How was it that he had the Ark? The firstborn seemed certain, yet wouldn't they have kept it with themselves? When the caravan had been attacked at the rear, the head of his personal guard had ordered them to the boats, the rest of the procession hurrying to follow with the carts.

But the Israelites had remained behind, as brothers, to fight.

And that meant their own cargo had remained with them.

So, if that were the case, why did his men end up with the Ark?

Tamrin, the head of his personal guard, jogged toward him, coming to a stop. "Your Highness, I have answers to your questions."

"Proceed."

"After questioning the men, I've discovered that a cart was brought forward by the Israelites last night while we rested. The next morning, four of them were in our midst, with no explanation beyond that they wanted to get to know us—some sort of goodwill gesture, I suppose."

Menelik frowned. "Why do I somehow doubt that?"

Tamrin agreed. "When the caravan was attacked, the four Israelites headed for the rear to join their brothers, then when the order was given to make haste for the boats, our men took the cart with them. None are aware of what is on it." He pointed to a dozen men approaching, carrying a shrouded box, there little doubt in Menelik's mind what was under it. "As you can see, they found the item." Tamrin paused. "May I ask what it is? I thought I heard the Israelite say it was the Ark of the Covenant? What is that?"

Menelik ignored the question, instead rushing toward the Ark. "Don't touch it except by the handles!"

His men froze, confused, all looking to see what they were holding on to, all relieved to see they were already following his orders.

"Put it down and look away!"

They complied, and Menelik carefully took a corner of the heavy cloth covering the Ark and lifted it, nearly fainting at the confirmation of what was among their midst.

What do I do?

This belonged to his father. To the Israelites. To their god. *His* god. It had to be returned, but the unloaded boats were already setting sail, their captains eager to return to the open seas or the safety of a port, his

121

own captain warning him that these were Egyptian lands, and they wouldn't take kindly to a small force landing on their shores outside of a port controlled by them where an inspection could occur.

It was that exact reason he had ordered the diversion, and it had been a wise move. If the Ark had been discovered by the Egyptians, there was no telling what might happen. But now that he had confirmed it was indeed among them, he had to return it, for there was no way God would want it with him, and not in Jerusalem where it could protect His chosen people.

"Sir! Look!"

He turned to find many of his men already staring to the north, hundreds of soldiers on horseback or war-carriage, supported by even more on foot.

"We must have been spotted bypassing the port," said Tamrin, giving orders with waves of his arms for the men to prepare to repel the enemy. "They must have sent a contingent to see where we landed."

Menelik cursed. The captain had begged him to set ashore north of the port, but he had refused, instead ordering them farther south, hoping to avoid this very encounter.

He was a fool.

"There are too many of them," he muttered, surveying the situation as his men readied themselves. "We can't win."

Tamrin shook his head. "No, sir, we can't. Only a miracle could save us now"—he gestured toward the departed boats—"or those returning."

Menelik grunted. "If you thought it was difficult to get them here the first time…"

122

Tamrin chuckled. "You're correct, of course, sir." He glanced at his liege. "What should we do?"

Menelik frowned. "Pray for that miracle."

Then a thought struck him, a thunderbolt of energy sending shivers through his body as he turned toward the Ark sitting only paces away.

"Perhaps a miracle is exactly what we need."

"Sir?"

Menelik gestured toward the Ark. "According to my father, the Ark of the Covenant is the means in which his people harness the power of God to defeat all their enemies."

Tamrin's eyebrows rose. "That…thing can stop an army?"

Menelik nodded. "Apparently so."

"How?"

Menelik's shoulders slumped. "I have no idea, and even if I did, I doubt it would work for us. It was, after all, stolen, and never was supposed to be in our possession."

Tamrin turned to face him. "Sir, if there's any chance that thing can work, we have to try, otherwise you will die."

Menelik regarded the army amassing in front of them, then checked their rear. They could flee, but they'd be forced to abandon their supplies, and this was Egyptian land. Eventually, they would be caught and slaughtered, and the Ark would fall into their hands, perhaps to be used against their traditional enemy, the Jewish people his father ruled.

You must try.

He closed his eyes, praying for some sort of message, some indication from the Jewish god of what he should do.

A strong breeze swept over him, cooling and calming, and he tingled all over, a smile spreading.

Thank you.

His eyes snapped open and he strode toward the Ark. "Have your men fall back and hold their position. Select ten of your bravest men to join us."

Tamrin's eyes widened. "Umm, forgive me, sir, but do you propose *twelve* of us face that army?"

Menelik shook his head. "No, my friend, there will be thirteen of us."

"Thirteen?"

"*God* will be with us."

John F. Kennedy International Airport

New York City, New York

Present Day

"There's nothing to be done here."

Fida regarded Ganno for a moment, the man in charge of their order since the death of his father almost twenty years ago. "So, you think the secret has been contained?"

Ganno nodded. "To the extent that no one beyond the professors know, yes. We'll deal with them when they've completed what has been asked of them by Father Amanuel."

"You're going to let them complete their work?"

"Of course, why wouldn't we?"

"Well, I thought our entire purpose was its destruction."

Ganno shook his head vehemently. "Then you're a fool! The Ark is the holiest of all relics, and was a gift from God Himself. We have no desire to destroy it, and you should know that!"

Fida stared at his leader, unable to believe what he was hearing. "But it is our sworn duty!"

"No, our sworn duty is to preserve its secret. For thousands of years, mankind has believed it to have been destroyed or at least lost forever. Everyone assumes it will never be found, and most probably believe it never existed. This is our Lord's will. And eventually, when man is united under one God, with the seat of power in Jerusalem, the prophecy will be fulfilled as our Lord predicted. But for that to happen, there must be no Ark to be worshipped. Should its existence be revealed, even for a brief moment in time, all the progress made to date will be lost."

"But that prophecy is only two thousand years old! Our mandate was given to us by Menelik himself, to the greatest grandfather Tamrin, with instructions to destroy it should it be discovered."

Ganno calmed slightly. "Yes, that is true, and is still true. But, my son, can you imagine if one nation today had the Ark? What would other nations do to stop them after its power was demonstrated in battle? We could see nuclear Armageddon. The end times. *That* is why we were mandated to destroy it should our religious leaders fail in their duty. We can never let it fall into the hands of those who might use it for evil purposes."

"But what of the prophecy? Doesn't that change everything?"

"Of course not! Jesus never said the Ark must not exist for mankind to unite. He merely said that man must have forgotten about it, that it would no longer be something that made man believe in Him, because an object would no longer be necessary to have faith."

Fida's head bobbed slowly as the teachings that had faded with his isolated life in America returned. "In other words, they must not be using it as a sign of God's power, but instead merely have faith in God's power without any symbols or icons to bolster it."

Ganno smiled, patting him on the shoulder. "Exactly, my son. Whether it is destroyed or not is irrelevant."

Fida frowned. "Then why not just destroy it?"

"Because it isn't God's will. He knows what our task is. If He wanted us to destroy it, he would force the priests into breaking their vows, thus compelling us to act."

Fida regarded him for a moment, not sure why the man didn't see what was so obvious. "Don't you think that's exactly what has happened here?"

Ganno stared at him for a moment, then sighed. "Perhaps. And if it has, then we'll take the action we have sworn to do. But remember, our first job is containment. If simply killing these professors is enough to preserve the secret, then that's what we'll do. Destroying the Ark is only a last resort." He opened the car door, shaking Fida's hand. "It is time for me to return home. Praise be to Menelik and Tamrin, and to our Lord, Jesus Christ."

Fida returned the blessing, then pulled away from the unloading zone of JFK International. He drove for several minutes before getting stopped by a red light. He fished his phone from his pocket and brought up his messages.

A smile spread.

I'm going to have more money than Menelik himself!

127

Acton/Palmer Residence

St. Paul, Maryland

Lee Fang let Acton's best friend and boss, Gregory Milton, unlock the door to the professors' residence, then motioned for him to step back. She expected the house to be empty, but she was having the most fun she had had in weeks if not longer.

I miss this so much.

She had been a major in the Chinese People's Liberation Army, part of the Beijing Military Region Special Forces Unit, which had meant constant training and constant action. Now she was an exile, wanted by the government she once served, and all alone in this strange new land, until Kane had reached out to her with an olive branch and a kind word.

And they had fallen in love.

She smiled as she entered the humble home, a surprise since the Actons were apparently worth hundreds of millions, Laura having inherited a fortune from her Internet tycoon brother when he died. Yet this home screamed middle-class America.

"The alarm is still on. Are you sure someone broke in?"

She nodded. "They reenabled it when they left."

Milton keyed in his code, the alarm chirping then going silent.

Sherrie White stepped deeper into the professors' home, her weapon drawn. "They obviously didn't want anyone to know they had been here."

"Looks like they did a good job," said Milton. "It doesn't look like anything's been touched."

Fang quickly swept the main floor while Sherrie cleared the second. She turned to Milton. "Where's their computer?"

Milton shook his head. "They use laptops. They take them wherever they go."

Sherrie returned. "We're clear. No evidence of anyone being here, but we might want to do a bug sweep, just in case."

Fang handed her the bag containing their equipment, the experienced CIA agent quickly going to work. "Any idea why they're in Ethiopia?"

Milton eyed her. "How did you know where they were?"

Sherrie glanced over her shoulder as she continued her sweep for eavesdropping devices. "We're the CIA. We know everything."

Fang grunted. "Well, I'm not, but Dylan and Sherrie are."

Milton chuckled. "The way you hold that gun, if you're not CIA, then you're just some other acronym."

A wave of nostalgic regret washed over Fang and she turned away, pretending to search the room some more. She loved her life in America, she loved Kane, she loved the two friends she did have, Chris and Sherrie, but it was the fact she could list off her entire social circle with a digit challenged hand, that had her depressed too often. She had no family, no extended network of friends, and no prospects.

Not even a work family.

The American government provided her with a generous monthly allowance as a thank you for her sacrifice on their behalf, and it meant she didn't need to work. But it came with restrictions, including not working in any field that might require her to make use of her unique skill set.

And anything that might bring her attention to Beijing.

"Hey, are you okay?"

Milton's voice was gentle, concerned, and she wiped away an escaped tear she hadn't noticed.

"Yes." She didn't elaborate, her single word bereft of emotion, ending the conversation.

Sherrie returned, stuffing the bug detector into the bag. "The house is clean. I think they were looking for something and left."

Fang pointed to a pile of papers on the kitchen counter. "They ordered some equipment recently, including a diesel generator. It might have something to do with what's going on."

Sherrie examined the pile, photographing each page and sending it to Leroux and Kane. Her phone vibrated while she was transmitting the photos, and she smiled. "We've got something from a security camera across the street." She shook her head. "People really need to change their default passwords." She pulled up the footage and held the phone out for the others to see.

Fang leaned in, the footage showing two black men entering the house, then a jump in the timecode, and the same two men leaving.

"Well, they look out of place."

Fang regarded Milton. "Why? Is this a white neighborhood?"

Milton's eyes widened in horror. "No, that's not what I meant at all!" He pointed at one of the men in the footage. "What I meant was that one's clothing is clearly East African, and if Jim and Laura just went to Ethiopia, then that's too much of a coincidence."

Fang smiled, always finding it interesting how Americans were so quick to take offense to any perceived slight of a minority group, or defend themselves desperately against any misinterpretation of something completely innocent.

She noticed it all the time on the news or on social media, two things she had too much time to partake in, finding this national obsession fascinating. It was something that simply wasn't an issue in China. Political correctness hadn't caught on yet back home, nor did she see it ever being allowed to get out of control like it was here.

"What do you think?" asked Sherrie, zooming in on the man in question. "Too much of a coincidence?"

Fang nodded. "In New York City, maybe not, but here in St. Paul? Absolutely. This is definitely related to their trip."

Milton's head swiveled between the two women. "So, what now?"

Sherrie led them to the front door. "Now, you go home, report anything to us out of the ordinary, and we'll try to contact the professors to let them know what's happened."

"Can you identify the men?"

"If they can be, they will be. The way that one guy is dressed suggests he's either a recent immigrant, or here visiting, so there should be a record."

"Umm, you mentioned things out of the ordinary."

Sherrie stopped and turned to face the hesitant Milton. "Yes?"

"Well, umm, when Tommy hacked their phones to let me know where they were, I noticed that one of the last calls on Jim's phone was to Italy. Rome, I think."

Fang's eyes narrowed. "Does he know people there?"

Milton chuckled. "Well, he knows the Pope, if that counts. But there are others."

Sherrie reset the alarm. "Okay, we'll follow up on it."

They stepped outside and Milton closed the door behind them, locking it. "Do you want Tommy to get you that info?"

Sherrie smiled. "I'm sure our people can handle it."

Milton laughed. "Of course." He sighed. "I'm glad you're on the job. I'll rest a little easier." He shook both their hands then climbed in his car and drove away.

Sherrie laughed and Fang looked at her. "What?"

"What he said about resting a little easier. Normally when people like us need to be on the job, it makes sleep more difficult."

Fang smiled at the truth in Sherrie's statement.

What an odd country.

Unknown Location

South of Aksum, Ethiopia

I give up.

Acton had tried desperately to keep track of the twists and turns as they had been transported, blindfolded, to where the genuine Ark of the Covenant was apparently kept. But it was no use. Half an hour of lefts and rights, ups and downs, some roads jarring, others as smooth as fresh pavement, had him completely lost.

For all he knew, they could be back where they started, or in New Jersey.

The vehicle skidded to a halt and the engine turned off. Doors opened and Acton flinched at Father Amanuel's voice to his left. "We're here. Watch your step."

A hand on his forearm helped him out of the vehicle, then he was led somewhere for about twenty penguin paces before being brought to a halt.

"There's a set of stairs, like before. Be careful."

"This would be a lot safer without the blindfolds," said Laura from behind him.

"Agreed."

"Don't worry. Once we reach the bottom, you can take them off. We can't risk you seeing any of the surrounding area. It's for your own safety."

"How?" asked Acton. "You keep saying stuff like that. Who are you trying to keep us safe from?"

"It does not matter."

"I think it does."

"If you knew, it would only increase the danger. Now, follow me, carefully."

The hand on Acton's forearm gently pulled him forward, and he inched ahead, finding the first step. It truly was disconcerting, and it reminded him of a conversation where a student claimed he could drive and text at the same time without being distracted. Acton had challenged him to run down the stairs while texting, then led the class to the stairwell to watch the arrogant fool prove his point by nearly breaking his neck.

Once below ground, he reached out with the other hand and touched the outer wall, giving him more confidence, though only a little. It seemed like an eternity doing this Bird Box style, but they were soon at the bottom where he was led inside, the area noticeably cooler.

"You can remove your blindfold now."

Acton did, sighing in relief and blinking to adjust his eyes. He turned to check on Laura, and smiled at her, reaching out his hand. She took it, then nodded toward the back of the room. Acton frowned at the sight of four men, armed with AKs, all wearing the robes of monks. "Not very Christian."

Amanuel chuckled. "They are volunteers who protect us from those who would take what we possess."

"Doesn't that mean you risk exposure from someone talking?"

Amanuel shrugged. "Who would believe them?"

"What if one of them gets greedy and decides to just shoot you?"

"They never know which is the real one."

Acton eyed the elderly priest. "Umm, don't they know now?"

Amanuel smiled. "None of them speak English."

"Are you sure?"

"Yes. We raise them from little boys, and never expose them to the language. They can be trusted to not understand what is going on. Beyond that, it is in God's hands."

"Well, guns make me nervous when they're not in *my* hands, because they usually end up shooting at me." Acton gestured toward the set of locked doors. "Can we see it?"

Amanuel bowed slightly. "Of course." He unlocked the doors and pushed them open, revealing a room remarkably similar to the one they had been in half an hour ago. Acton's heart was hammering anew, and he glanced at Laura as she squeezed his hand. Was this going to be another disappointment, another fake, meant to trick them once again? And how could they know either way without the proper equipment to test?

Maybe you'll just know.

They stepped inside and he frowned, unsure of what he had expected. The room was exactly as the other was, with an ark that appeared in every way the same as the other.

Except for one thing.

One of the poles meant to lift it was broken in half, only the gold cladding holding it together.

Laura let go of his hand and examined the exposed wood. "At least the wood is right this time. Acacia." She removed a measuring tape from her pocket, quickly taking measurements of the Ark itself, calling out the numbers, Acton performing the math in his head.

He smiled.

"Two-and-a-half cubits, by one-and-a-half, by one-and-a-half."

Laura nodded, returning the measuring tape to her satchel. "Exactly as described in Exodus."

Acton turned to Amanuel. "But how do we know it's actually the real one? This could just be a better fake."

Amanuel smiled. "You must have faith, my son."

Acton grunted. "I'm a scientist. I like to deal in facts."

Amanuel regarded him for a moment. "When it comes to God, don't you find that a little difficult?"

Acton sighed. "You got me there." He held out his hand, his fingers hovering inches over the gold top, the cherubim on either side. "There is one way to find out."

Laura gave him a look. "If God strikes you down, who the hell am I supposed to ask for retribution?"

Acton grinned. "Good question."

Amanuel approached, keeping a reverent distance from the relic. "Have you ever felt the power of God?"

Acton thought back at some of their escapades over the past several years, his mind settling on two things. The blood relics they had encountered, and the True Cross. He could honestly say he had experienced genuinely spiritual moments, almost rapturous in their intensity.

He nodded.

"Then take a moment. Set aside your doubts and consider your history. You are scientists. You know the stories of Solomon and the Queen of Sheba, Makeda. You know they had a child together, Menelik. You know the Ark disappeared from Jerusalem. There are several theories as to how, but one is that the firstborn sons, sent with Menelik, stole it. Do you not believe that it is at least possible that these stories are true, and that the Ark has been here all along? Do you really believe a reputable officer like Ullendorff would have reported what he did?"

"He recanted."

"Yes, but not for years, and we can safely assume it was so he wouldn't be remembered as a laughing stock, for our deceptions had worked, with so many churches claiming to have the genuine article."

Acton glanced at Laura. "Reminds me of the Triarii."

Laura agreed. "It does, doesn't it? And it worked for them for two thousand years. Why not three thousand for these guys?"

Amanuel smiled. "You misunderstand. We merely hid the Ark for many generations. Subterfuge wasn't necessary until the last century, after Lieutenant Ullendorff's accidental exposure. Once the word was out, we were forced to go beyond simply hiding the Ark. We had to make it seem ridiculous that we had it."

Acton stepped back from the Ark, turning to face their host. "So, those with the fakes know they are fake, but don't know there actually is a real one out there?"

"Exactly. Very few know the truth. With dozens of churches making the claim to attract worshippers and donations, there would simply be too many involved for the secret to remain so."

Acton grunted. "We know man landed on the moon because there were too many involved for the secret to be kept if it weren't true."

Amanuel shrugged. "I know nothing of these things, but I believe you to be correct." He lowered his voice. "I sense you still have doubts."

"I do."

"*We* do," agreed Laura.

"Then I will tell you something that is known to fewer still. You *can* touch the Ark."

Acton's eyes shot wide. "You can? But doesn't that contradict the Bible?"

Amanuel shook his head. "No. The Bible says nothing of the consequences of touching the Ark, simply that it shouldn't be done. We, the Keepers, have discovered through accidents over the generations, that touching the Ark doesn't kill, as many feared, but instead does something to a man that is so profound, some may wish they had died instead of having experienced it."

Acton stared at him skeptically. "What do you mean by profound?"

Amanuel held up his hands. "I myself have never experienced it, as I am too much the coward. But I know of others who have touched it, and the experience drove some mad, and profoundly changed others."

"Changed them how?"

"I'm not sure how to describe it, exactly, as no one really speaks of it afterward, insisting anyone who wants to know must experience it for themselves." Amanuel stepped closer to Acton, stretching his hand toward the Ark. "I invite you to touch it, so any doubts you have will be removed, and we can continue with the task at hand."

Acton turned to Laura who shook her head. "Don't do it."

His eyebrows rose. "Why? You don't really think what he's saying is true, do you?"

"What if it is? Are you willing to take that risk?"

Acton was surprised to hear his wife of all people expressing these fears. "Listen, while I may believe in God, I don't believe in a God that will kill me or drive me insane simply by touching something. The God I believe in is good, not vengeful." He pointed at the Ark. "This Old Testament stuff was meant to strike fear. I'm more of a New Testament guy." He sucked in a deep breath. "Wish me luck."

Laura lunged to stop him, but it was too late. He gripped the cherubim, one in each hand.

And felt nothing.

He closed his eyes then gasped.

Kingdom of Ethiopia

10th Century BC

Forty Years Later

To say that Menelik was a true believer would be an understatement. He had witnessed the power of God firsthand. Though perhaps that wasn't entirely accurate. He had witnessed the *results* of the power of God firsthand. It had been decades since that fateful day on the shores of the Red Sea, but he remembered it like it was yesterday, and it still filled him with terror and reverence.

Their fates had been sealed, but when he and the others carried the Ark, uncovered, into the battle, he had said a silent prayer, then ordered his men to close their eyes, and keep them closed, no matter what they heard.

He had checked them all as the Egyptian army charged toward them, and with the first spears in the air, he had closed his own, and prayed for the miracle necessary to save them.

And when he opened his eyes only minutes later, after what felt like the most vicious of storms had pounded the area around them, the sounds of holy war unlike anything he could have imagined, nor described today, all had fallen silent, and all that remained on the battlefield were him and his companions, the Ark of the Covenant, and the beasts of war the Egyptians had been riding.

Nothing more.

The soldiers were gone, as were their weapons.

Nothing beyond their beasts were left to suggest they had ever been there.

Not even a single drop of blood.

"Open your eyes."

Tamrin opened a single eye, tentatively, then both. "Where did they go?"

Menelik shook his head. "I have no idea. God must have taken them."

"God?" Tamrin shuddered. "If your Jewish god can do this, then I've been worshipping the wrong god."

Menelik nodded. "Never before have I even *heard* of anything such as this, let alone witnessed it."

"What do we do?"

"We thank Him, then get ourselves home as quickly as possible."

Tamrin reached out for the Ark. "With this, we can take our time. We are unbeatable!"

Menelik slapped Tamrin's hand away. "What did I say? Never touch the Ark!"

Tamrin bowed. "I'm sorry, sir, I forgot." He took a healthy step back. "But with this, nobody can hurt us. Imagine what we could do when we return home? We would only need to enter battle once, and word would spread among our enemies that we are never to be touched again." His chest heaved with the excitement, his eyes widening with thoughts of the power they now wielded. "We could conquer them all!"

And it was then that Menelik knew what had just saved them, had also cursed them. For just because one could defeat one's enemies, one shouldn't necessarily do so. Using the Ark for defense was one thing, but for offense was something entirely different.

It was a responsibility that had haunted him for decades as king.

"How are you feeling today, my king?"

Menelik flinched, snapped from his reverie by his oldest and most trusted friend, Tamrin, no longer the head of his personal guard, that position now occupied by his friend's grandson, as it had been by his son after he was of sufficient age and experience.

It was a dynasty that had served the kingdom well, as Menelik's own son would continue his family's after his death, a death no longer on the horizon, but merely over the next hill.

"The same as yesterday, which is to say not good."

Tamrin frowned. "You should follow the example set by your mother. She abdicated the throne to you upon your return from the Holy Land, and now it is time for you to do the same."

Menelik nodded, his neck spasming. Everything hurt now, everything felt old now. "To be young again."

Tamrin grunted. "We've both lived good lives. It's time to make room for those who would follow us and see if they can improve upon what we've done."

Menelik frowned. "Do you think our sons will do better? Our grandsons?"

Tamrin regarded him for a moment, then took a seat beside him. "I hope so, though I have my doubts. My son told me just last night that my grandson asked him where the Ark is, and why it hasn't been used for so long." He frowned. "I got the sense he felt it was being asked on behalf of another."

"*My* grandson."

"It was only a sense."

"Unfortunately, I think you're correct in your suspicions. While my son and heir understands the horrific powers of the Ark, for he saw it the last time it was used, my grandson has never seen it, and I fear, once he has the power to command it, he will use it on our enemies, to conquer them once and for all." He shook his head. "The innocent shouldn't suffer under the power we wield. Let our enemies be, and as long as they do the same, there is no need for the Ark."

"Perhaps we should return it to the Israelites."

Menelik sighed. "I've thought of that. If they believed we still had it, then I'm certain they would have sent an army to retrieve it, but I believe our spies are correct, and that they think the Egyptians or the Philistines have it."

"Because there was no record of us putting to port."

"Exactly. They must believe that there is no record because the Egyptians want to hide the fact they confiscated it from us, or because we never made it home with it, a Philistine raiding party seizing it. Either way, we don't have it, and my father obviously decided not to pursue it any further, at least where we are concerned."

"Then why not return it?"

"I don't think God wants me to."

"Excuse me?" Tamrin eyed him. "Have you been hearing voices?"

Menelik chuckled. "No, I haven't, thank you, but don't you think if God didn't want us to have the Ark, he wouldn't have allowed us to keep it in the first place? Not to mention the fact he let us use it to defend ourselves on multiple occasions."

Tamrin nodded. "It is true that I've often thought about this. He clearly demonstrated His power on our behalf whenever we needed it."

"Then I suggest He doesn't want the Israelites to have it. After all, most of our people now worship Him, so are we any less chosen than the Israelites?"

Tamrin grunted. "That might be stretching it."

Menelik laughed. "Perhaps, though there is some truth there." He leaned closer to his friend. "Lately, I have been thinking that the decision should be left in God's hands."

"How?"

"I don't believe any man should wield such power unless it is the will of God."

"Agreed, but clearly it was His will that allowed that power to be wielded on our behalf, and that of its previous owners."

"Yes, but think about it. The Jews needed the Ark to protect them while they were weak. Now they are strong. Do they really need it anymore? And look at us. We didn't ask for the Ark, we didn't steal it, yet just when we needed it, we discovered we had it." He regarded his friend. "Remember that day? You found it and brought it to me, then only moments later the Egyptian army was spotted. *Moments* later. What if they had shown up just five minutes earlier? We wouldn't be sitting here today, and the Egyptians would have marched across half the known world by now with such power. Instead, it was revealed to us the very moment we needed it, and saved us, and eventually our people, when our enemies dared attack after my mother's abdication. They thought we were weak, and they were proven wrong. *I* believe the Ark will find a way to help those who need it most, and right now, that isn't us *or* the Israelites."

"If not us, then who?"

Menelik shrugged. "I have no idea. That is for God to decide."

"Then what do we do in the meantime? If your grandson is agitating for its use, once you die, he may just win out."

"That is why I've summoned the rabbis to meet with me later. The Ark is to be placed in hiding until God's will reveals it to whoever may be in need."

Tamrin's jaw dropped. "Your grandson will tear the kingdom apart to find it."

Menelik nodded. "He will, but the plan the rabbis and I have come up with is, I think, sound." He reached out and took his friend's arm. "It is you and your family's task that will be much more difficult."

146

Tamrin tensed. "What do you have in store for us?"

"The most difficult task of all. A task that may last until the end of days."

Bedford Park, New York City
Present Day

Fida smiled at the sight, then quickly angled his laptop so none of the Starbucks customers walking by could see what had him so excited. Normally he wouldn't be on the Dark Web in such a public place, but he had no choice.

His neighbor had finally enabled his wi-fi security, and he hadn't had time to find a new unsecured connection.

But that was all about to change.

Soon he could afford his own dedicated gigabit connection.

Dozens of queries for more information were in his secure email, demanding specifics beyond what he had posted as his teaser earlier. Many appeared serious, others were from what sounded like religious zealots rather than collectors, and still others from trolls.

He needed to somehow separate the serious bidders.

Bidders.

He smiled, quickly typing a new message to append to his original posting.

I know where the item Menelik took from Solomon is located. If you know your history, and are serious, deposit USD 10,000 in the account below.

He posted the account number where the Sons of Tamrin deposited his monthly stipend, an account in the Caymans the others couldn't do anything with beyond deposit money, then brought up the website where he could see the pittance of a balance available to him.

Then gulped as the first deposit appeared, then another and another. Before he had finished his coffee, he had more money than he had seen in his entire life.

His pulse raced with the implications. These were criminals, in the business, who would kill him if he didn't come through.

A single bead of sweat trickled down his spine.

He snapped the laptop shut.

What have I done?

What had been fantasy was now reality. Serious people had paid serious money, and now he had to deliver. Yet all he could do was provide the names of those that would lead these people to the Ark.

Professors James Acton and Laura Palmer.

The rest would be up to the highest bidder.

Operations Center 3, CIA Headquarters

Langley, Virginia

"I've got hits on our two suspects."

Chris Leroux turned in his chair located at the heart of one of the CIA's state-of-the-art operations centers. From here, he and his team of analysts could tap any source of information around the world, run clandestine operations, monitor world affairs and military movements, and pretty much create any havoc they might want.

As long as they had been granted the authority to do so, of course.

"Who are they?" he asked his youngest team member and computer wunderkind, Randy Child.

"The first guy in the garb is Dawit Ganno. He's traveling on an Ethiopian passport. Arrived from London, departed JFK earlier today, heading back to Ethiopia. The other one is Asrat Fida. He's an immigrant originally from Ethiopia. He has his citizenship, and works as a janitor at the Ethiopian Orthodox Tewahedo Church of Our Savior in the Bronx. No criminal record, files his taxes, looks clean."

Leroux pursed his lips, folding his arms. "Okay, we need to know why these two have taken an interest in the professors, and what the professors are doing in Ethiopia. The Chief has authorized us to find out what we can from the confines of this room. No external resources, at least for now. Not until we confirm they're in trouble."

Child grunted. "They usually are."

"True, but the Chief wants to give them the benefit of the doubt today."

"He's optimistic," said Sonya Tong, his senior analyst.

"I guess his glass is half full today," offered Child.

"Woke up on the right side of the bed?"

"Got some last night?"

Groans greeted Child's last one.

He spun in his chair, looking at the others. "What? Did that one cross the line?"

Tong gave him the eye. "Ya think?"

Child nodded. "Okay, note to self. No jokes about the Chief's sex life."

"Anyone's sex life," added Leroux.

"Amended note. Anyone's sex life." He grinned. "Including mine?"

"You have to have one to joke about it," muttered Tong.

"Ouch!"

Tong high-fived one of the others as laughter rippled through the room.

Child, red-faced, pointed at her. "It's on like Donkey Kong!"

Leroux shook his head. "No, it's not. Trace our Ethiopians' movements, and the professors. I want to know what they're doing in Ethiopia with that equipment they ordered, and why these two felt it was necessary to break into their home and apparently take nothing."

Marseilles, France

"Hey, Alexie, something interesting is going on."

Alexie Tankov glanced up from his tablet at his second-in-command, Arseny Utkin. "What?"

Utkin sat beside him, the pool of their villa on the French Riviera filled with a bevy of beauties in all shapes and colors, the rest of the team either playing a game of volleyball with them, or in various states of coitus around the deck.

It was a good life.

Far better than the Spetsnaz days.

"Looks like some guy is claiming he knows where the Ark of the Covenant is."

Tankov tore his eyes away from a particularly voluptuous Nubian girl who had no boundaries whatsoever. "Really? He actually said that?"

"Well, no, but he claims to know how to find what Menelik took from Solomon."

Tankov sat up, spinning his legs off the lounger. "An interesting way to put it."

"I paid the buy-in for the bid. Just ten thousand. The guy's obviously an idiot and hasn't got a clue what he's doing. People would pay ten times that just for a shot at getting their hands on the Ark."

"Or he's a genius who just bilked dozens out of ten grand each, and he'll disappear into the ether by morning."

Utkin frowned. "So, what do you want me to do?"

"I'll make some calls. I don't want to waste our money bidding on dust, but if there's any chance of this being for real, it could be worth hundreds of millions."

Utkin eyed him. "The Sheikh? He's not very happy with us right now, not since we tipped off the Americans and he lost most of his collection."

"Yeah, but he doesn't know it was us."

"He probably suspects it though."

"True, but something like this could make us square with him again, and he was our best buyer."

Utkin nodded. "Only if it's real."

"Agreed." Tankov grabbed his phone. "Start monitoring the usual haunts, and pull together anything you can find on this Menelik/Solomon link to the Ark."

"You got it." Utkin rose and headed back inside as Tankov dialed his favorite customer that currently hated him.

"Sheik Khalid, I'm pleased to hear your voice. I was concerned you may have fallen out of favor in your kingdom."

He was greeted with a growl. "You have a lot of nerve calling me."

"You aren't still sore about losing the Amber Room, are you?"

"If I ever find out it was you, you'll rue the day you met me."

Tankov smiled. "Trust me, if what I might have found for you is real, you'd forgive me even if I had defiled all your wives."

"What have you found?"

The eagerness and greed were obvious to anyone, and Tankov's smile spread.

All is forgiven.

Milton Residence

St. Paul, Maryland

Milton couldn't take it any longer, his back aching, his fingers fidgeting, his mind so preoccupied with thoughts of his friends, he hadn't accomplished a lick of work all day.

He grabbed his phone and called Tommy Granger.

"Anything?"

"No, not yet."

Milton cursed, then decided a line needed to be crossed now that there was a criminal element involved with the break-in. "Do you still have his call history?"

"Yup."

"There was a call to Italy. Give me the number."

There was a pause as keys were tapped. "Well, look at that. How did you know?"

"I saw it on your screen."

"Good eye, Deano. Well, umm, are you sure you want to do this? I thought you didn't want to violate their privacy."

"Just give it to me!"

"Umm, yes, sir." Tommy's reply was meek, and Milton immediately regretted snapping at the kid.

"Listen, Tommy, I'm sorry. I'm just scared for my friends. This is getting more serious than we first thought."

"Why? What's happened?"

"I can't say. In fact, I think it's best if you back off. We'll let the pros handle this one."

There was another pause. "Pros, huh? As in, umm, *pros?*"

"Exactly."

Tommy whistled. "So, this *is* serious."

"It could be."

"Then do you really want me to stop digging? I mean, I've helped these *pros* out before."

Milton shook his head. "You're going to no matter what I say, aren't you?"

"So, you *do* know me!"

Milton groaned. "Fine. Just keep a low profile."

"I always do."

"Good. Now give me that number."

Milton jotted it down then ended the call, immediately dialing Italy, his breath held.

"Giasson."

Milton sighed in relief, his suspicions confirmed. "Hi, M. Giasson. This is Gregory Milton, Jim Acton's friend."

"Yes, of course, Dean Milton of St. Paul's University. What can I do for you?"

"Well, I'm not sure how to say this, but, well, I'm concerned Jim and Laura may have stepped into it again, so I had someone pull their phone records, and noticed Jim called you."

"Yes."

Milton sensed some hesitation. "I was wondering if you know what they're doing in Ethiopia."

There was a long pause, and Milton wondered if the line was still connected. "I got the sense Jim didn't want anyone to know we spoke, but if he's in trouble—"

"I think he is. Two people broke into their house soon after they left, and took nothing. It was as if they were searching for something."

"That's disconcerting." Giasson sighed. "I can't tell you much, Greg, but I can tell you what I suspect."

Milton tensed. "And that is?"

"I think they may have found the Ark of the Covenant."

Bedford Park, New York City

Fida sat in a corner booth and horribly failed at suppressing his grin as his wallet, bulging with cash for the first time in his life, dug itself into his bony ass.

He reveled in the discomfort.

Just with the buy-ins deposited, he was already richer than most in his homeland, but this was only the tip of the iceberg.

When this is done, I'm going north to see an actual iceberg, and never feel the heat of the desert again.

He frowned. After over a decade of living in New York City, he had experienced every form of weather he could imagine, including the shock of a cold winter, and hated to admit it to himself, but he did miss the heat of his homeland. While the winters were fun the first few times, they quickly became annoying and something he hated after time.

Now I can afford to head south to avoid them.

He grunted, taking a sip of his upscale coffee, no expense spared this time, his regular barista asking him if he had won the lottery.

In a sense, he had.

But he had to keep his mouth shut in this neighborhood. Flashing Benjamins could mean a knife in the gut or a bullet to the back of the head.

Just like back home.

He opened his backpack, removing the bottles of water piled on top, then pulled out his laptop. He returned the bottles to his pack, remembering when he had first arrived here from the wilds of his meager existence, and how he had marveled at the tap in his apartment that had an endless supply of clean, cool water. It had been one of the most fascinating and unexpected things he had discovered in his new home.

There's something to be said about never being thirsty.

And he was rarely hungry. If he budgeted wisely, he was well fed, though sometimes, near the end of the month, things turned a little meager in quality. He always found it ridiculous that it was more expensive to eat healthy in America, than it was to eat junk food.

One dollar hamburgers, six dollar salads.

He took another sip of his coffee as his laptop booted up, then positioned the screen so no one could see what he was doing.

Then took a bite of his muffin, something he hadn't had in months, treats like this a luxury he could ill afford.

He moaned aloud, eliciting giggles from the teenage girls at the next booth. He flushed, slouching in his seat as he logged in to the auction site.

His heart skipped a beat at the messages waiting from those who had already paid, demanding more concrete details otherwise there'd be consequences.

This was a mistake.

He shifted in his seat, the bulge of a thousand dollars in cash reminding him of why he was doing this, and why he couldn't possibly stop.

Cash.

Money.

Enough to change his life.

He could walk away now. They'd never find him. But he wanted more. He wanted the American dream. He wanted to be rich, to never worry about going hungry or cold again, to never thirst for anything.

He wanted it all, the Ark be damned.

What did it matter? It was a forgotten relic from a forgotten time. His group's mandate was to destroy it should its discovery not be contained, so if it were okay to destroy it for those reasons, why shouldn't he be able to profit from it, then allow his brethren to destroy it when those who won the bid came to collect? All he was doing was ending millennia of waiting.

He posted a new message for those who had met the buy-in, uploading a redacted copy of the invoices they had discovered in the professors' home.

The item is as you suspected. The Ark of the Covenant. Note the measurements for the containment system. The people hired are experts in preserving ancient artifacts.

The winning bidder will get their names, and their last known location. Find them, and you will find the Ark. Deposit USD 100,000 to qualify within the next four hours.

His eyes bulged as within minutes, every single bidder had paid the second deposit. He was now a millionaire, and again could walk away.

But now he wanted it all.

He posted another message.

Deposits received. Bidding starts at USD 1,000,000 and ends in 4 hours.

He sat back and closed his eyes, dreaming of the millions he would have before the day was out.

Unknown Location

South of Aksum, Ethiopia

At first, Acton felt nothing. The anticlimactic moment shouldn't have surprised him. After all, the likelihood of this being the real Ark of the Covenant was infinitesimal. In fact, he wasn't even convinced there ever was an Ark, and if there was, it certainly didn't have the power of God at its beck and call.

Then he thought of the priest's words about having faith and letting go of the scientist within. He closed his eyes, drawing a deep breath as he tried to clear his mind. He believed in God. At least he thought he did. Whether it was the God from the Bible, he wasn't sure. While many things in the Bible had been proven historically, those were events such as battles or particular leaders being in power. Nothing supernatural or godlike had ever been proven. Those were the types of things that had to be witnessed firsthand.

Yet he had always wondered how, in a time when there was no Internet, little writing, and no forms of modern communication, a man could wander into a town, speak to the people, then leave for the next town, and have his deeds talked about enough that within a few hundred years, the greatest empire the world had ever known had converted to worship him.

Yes, the words might have been inspiring, but they were just words. Give a good speech, move on, people talk about you for a few days, maybe a few weeks, but you're quickly forgotten.

Heal the blind, the crippled, the diseased, or raise the dead, then move on, people talk about you for the rest of their lives.

He felt a spark.

Something deep down, in his stomach, the unease of anticipation, like the excitement one might feel waiting for a terrifying rollercoaster ride, both excited and nervous at what was to come. The sensation spread, washing over him, his breathing increasing as his entire body tingled.

What's happening?

It was terrifying, it was exhilarating, it was overwhelming. He didn't know what was going on, but he had never felt this way before. Was it in his head? Was it something he was creating himself?

Or was it in his soul, delivered to him by God Himself?

And as he imagined what it must have been like for the Israelites thousands of years ago, carrying this holy artifact into battle and witnessing its awesome might, the true power of their god, he could sense the emotions they must have felt, the fear, the awe, the rapturous joy of unbridled faith.

It was too much.

He forced himself to let go and collapsed to his knees, his chest heaving, tears flowing down his cheeks as Laura rushed to his side.

"Are you okay?"

He wasn't. A pit rapidly formed in his stomach, a wave of nausea surging through him as his heart continued to race. He fell to his side, lying on his back, his vision blurred as Laura leaned over him, her words lost in a fog of disorientation as his heart threatened to give up from the strain.

It's in your stomach.

He closed his eyes, focusing on that small thread of knowledge as he battled through the panic of what he was certain was a heart attack.

It's in your stomach, not just your chest.

He drew a deep breath, holding it for a few seconds before exhaling. It wasn't a heart attack. It was a panic attack, manifesting itself in his stomach, creating a feedback loop that made his brain think he was dying, his heart hammering faster and faster in fear.

But it was all in his head.

He struggled to control his breathing, each breath slightly more governed, and he remembered his training from his stint in the National Guard.

Tactical breathing.

"Just calm down, you're okay."

It was Laura, her voice finally breaking through his panic, and he reached out for her, his hand clasped tightly a moment later, an anchor to reality. He continued his slow, rhythmic breathing, counting off the steps in his head, then blew a final breath through pursed lips.

"I'm okay."

She smiled down at him, wiping the tears off his cheeks. "You sure?"

"Yeah." He struggled to his feet, brushing himself off, his cheeks flushing as he realized how many had witnessed his embarrassing display. "I'm sorry. I'm, umm, well, not sure what happened there."

"You experienced the rapture."

Acton turned to Father Amanuel, the man smiling at him as if a wonderful experience had just been shared. "Is that what you call it?"

Laura clasped his hand to her chest, concern still on her face as he noticed three of her fingers were checking his pulse on his wrist. "What happened?"

"I-I'm not sure. At first, nothing, then I just began to feel things that became overpowering, overwhelming." He lowered his voice. "It was, I don't know how else to describe it, but it was spiritual. Religious, I guess? I know that's not very scientific, but for a moment, it felt like I was experiencing the emotions of those who had carried it into battle thousands of years ago. It was as if I was there." He shuddered, turning toward the Ark, its gleaming gold now with an aura around it he hadn't noticed before. Was it in his head? Was he just imagining it?

Or was it real?

Another surge of emotion and adrenaline rushed through him, his entire body tingling with the excitement of the truth he wanted to believe had just been revealed.

"I-I think it's real!"

Granger/Trinh Residence

St. Paul, Maryland

Tommy Granger sat against a propped up pillow, Mai lying beside him watching Game of Thrones yet again as he searched the darkest recesses of the Internet for any clue as to what the professors were doing in Ethiopia. He was concerned. When Mai had helped them escape Vietnam, she had been forced to come with them, and they had been her family since. And when he had started dating Mai, they had embraced him as well.

He almost thought of them as his parents, and he knew Mai felt the same way.

They were good people. The best. And he wanted to help them in any way possible.

And so far, he had come up empty.

Mai's hand drifted to his nether regions.

"Hon, I'm trying to work."

She gave him a squeeze. "You better be done by the time this episode is finished."

He glanced at the screen, someone doing someone in earnest. "Uh huh."

"You know how horny this show makes me."

"It's not the show. It's Jason Momoa. You couldn't keep your hands off me after Aquaman." He eyed her. "In fact, you couldn't keep your hands off me *during* Aquaman."

She grinned. "You didn't seem to mind."

He shrugged. "I'm a dude." He pushed her face back toward her own laptop. "Now back to your show. I've got—"

His phone rang and he glanced at the display. "It's the Dean." He pointed at her show. "Pause that." He swiped his thumb as Mai clicked pause. "Hello, sir."

"Hi, Tommy, I hope I didn't wake you."

"You didn't."

"Good. I've got something to add to your Internet monitoring."

Tommy sat up a little straighter. "What?"

"The Ark of the Covenant."

Tommy's eyes shot wide. "Are you serious? Like in the movie?"

"Nooo, like in the Bible."

Tommy flushed. "Oh yeah, right. Okay." A thought occurred to him. "Wait! Do you think they found it?"

"I don't know, just check it out and let me know."

"Will do. And if I find something?"

"Call me. Day or night."

168

"Okay."

The call ended and he attacked his keyboard, feeding the new search criteria into his program busy crawling every corner he could think of, and his heart skipped a beat as a hit appeared, then dozens, all surrounding a discussion group about an illegal art auction site.

"Uh oh."

Mai looked at him. "What?"

But he ignored her, instead dialing Milton back.

"Already?"

"Yes, sir. We, umm, might have a problem."

"What?"

He could hear the concern in Milton's voice, well aware that Acton was the man's best friend for over twenty years. "There's talk of some joker, their word, claiming he knows where the Ark is, and wants ten grand to bid on the info. I found the site. He's making reference to Solomon and Menelik, which according to what I read, refers to the Queen of Sheba and how her son Menelik took the Ark with him to Ethiopia."

"Could be just a coincidence. Maybe somebody is claiming that every day."

"I don't think so. It was just posted today, and I didn't find anything else that was recent. There seems to be quite a bit of buzz around this, so I'm thinking it's unusual."

"Can you tell who posted it?"

"Nothing beyond a random username, but the guy isn't very good at this. He posted his bank account info in the post for the buy-in."

"That doesn't sound too bright."

"It isn't."

"Okay, send it to me. I'll call the pros."

Unknown Location

South of Aksum, Ethiopia

"You're okay. It will pass. Just breathe. In and out, slowly. In and out, slowly."

Acton held Laura as she sat on the floor in his arms, the love of his life having insisted on experiencing the Ark herself, her reaction, from all outward appearances, the same as his.

She closed her eyes and drew a loud breath through her nose, then exhaled slowly, nodding. "Okay, I think it's over."

Acton helped her to her feet then moved the hair from her face with the end of his finger. "You okay?"

"Yes, just a little frazzled. That was intense."

"What was it like for you?"

She turned to face the Ark, shaking her head slowly. "It was odd. I didn't feel anything at first, but then as I began to think about what I *should* be feeling if it were real, I started to feel things. I found myself imagining the most horrific of things mixed with I'm not sure what. It was a confluence of emotions all at once. I don't know if it was all in my head, or if it was from the Ark, but it was intense."

Acton exhaled loudly. "You mean you think it could have been all in your head?"

She shrugged. "I don't know. It wouldn't be unprecedented. You go in believing something will happen, so your mind makes it happen."

Acton's stomach was suddenly cleaved hollow. Could she be right? Could it all have been in his head? He had wanted it to be real, he had wanted to experience something. Had his mind created what he wanted?

He turned to the priest. "I'm not so sure anymore."

Amanuel smiled. "You have to have faith, my son. Do you truly believe that you, a man of science, would have such a rapturous, overwhelming response, simply by touching something I told you was real? A devout believer? Absolutely. But a skeptic like yourself? Are you really that weak of mind that you think it was all in your head, your scientific, logical head?"

Laura leaned against Acton and rested her head on his shoulder. He stared down at her, and could see she was as confused as he was. He looked at Amanuel. "I don't know." He sighed. "I wouldn't think so."

Amanuel reached out, patting them both on the shoulder. "Then have faith. Both of you. You know yourselves, and I think, deep down, you know the truth. Your minds have both been touched by the hand of God Himself." He stared each of them in the eyes. "And you will never be the same."

Operations Center 3, CIA Headquarters

Langley, Virginia

"They're definitely building something."

Leroux agreed with Tong's assessment as the records of Laura Palmer's credit card purchases were cross-referenced with the invoices found at her home. A diesel generator was the most recognizable item beyond basic building supplies, but it was the other things that interested him. "I think this stuff is all used for climate control."

Child stared at the ceiling as he spun in his chair. "You mean like global warming?"

Tong eyed him. "Maybe if you stopped spinning in that chair of yours, you wouldn't be so dizzy and could think straight."

Child dropped a foot, halting his spin. "I spin both ways to balance it out."

"It doesn't work that way."

Child shrugged. "Does for me." He tapped some keys and specs for a basic box of some type appeared. "They're building some sort of preservation chamber for an archaeological find. You know, like those display cases you see in a museum." He grinned at Tong. "When I spin, we all win."

"Okay, Dr. Seuss. What are they preserving?"

"Well, they're archaeologists, so obviously something old and important that needs to be preserved." He shrugged. "Something made of wood?"

Leroux jumped in before the tone became nastier. "Possible. Stone wouldn't require something like this, I wouldn't think, but I'm no expert. And why the hurry unless it needed protection quickly?"

Tong agreed. "It was fast. This all happened in a matter of a couple of days. Maybe whoever asked for their help discovered they had a problem just recently."

"But who?" Leroux tapped his chin as he stared at the photos of their two suspects. "It can't be them. Why break into their house? It has to be someone else."

Child resumed his spin. "But how did they know? I mean, if they didn't hire them, then how did they know to go to the professors' house?"

Leroux shook his head. "I think all our answers are in Ethiopia. That's where the professors are, that's where the equipment they bought was taken, which means that's likely where whoever hired them is. It's also where one of our two suspects is heading." He turned to Tong. "And we have nothing on them after they arrived?"

174

Tong shook her head. "No, they arrived in Aksum, their cellphones pinged for a short while, then that's it. They left the city heading south."

"Curious that they didn't land in Addis Ababa."

"It's sixteen hours from where they landed. Obviously, their final destination is closer to Aksum."

Leroux clasped his hands behind his neck. "Okay, pull any satellite footage we have of the area. Maybe we'll get lucky. The equipment they brought with them had to have been transported on trucks, so if a bird happened to be going by, we might at least get a bearing on where they were headed."

Tong turned toward him. "Sir, I've got Gregory Milton on the line for you."

Leroux's eyebrows rose slightly then he positioned his headset, tapping the button to take the call and put it on speaker. "Dean Milton, this is Leroux. How can I help you?"

"Mr. Leroux, I've found out something you need to know."

There was both excitement and fear in the man's voice, and Leroux tensed slightly. "What's that?"

"I called that number in Italy."

"M. Giasson."

"Yes." There was a pause. "Umm, did you call him?"

"No, not yet. We're still gathering intel covertly on this end. What did he have to say?"

"He thinks Jim and Laura have, umm, found the Ark of the Covenant."

The entire room came to a halt, even a spinning Child.

"Ahh, can you repeat that?"

"He thinks they've found the Ark, you know, from the Bible. Moses, the Ten Commandments."

"Yes, sir, I'm fully aware of what the Ark is." Leroux stared at the invoices still on the main displays that occupied the entire front of the operations center, it all making sense. "Why does he think they found it?"

"He said Acton called him to check on a priest named Father Amanuel who visited them, wanting to hire them for a preservation job. This priest was the piece we've been missing. Mario, I mean M. Giasson, was able to look up the man and found he serves at the Church of Saint Mary of Zion in Ethiopia. He says that church is located in an area where a lot of them claim to have the Ark."

Leroux wasn't sure what to believe. After all, this was the Ark of the Covenant Milton was talking about. He had his doubts as to whether it had ever existed, or was just a story from the Bible meant to inspire and strike fear into the enemies of the Jewish people.

And the connection was tenuous. A priest who serves at a church that is in the *area* where *a lot* of churches claim to have the Ark? The entire thing screamed ridiculous.

But the professors were smart people. Very smart. Would they run off, telling no one where they were going or why, for something they didn't at least have a reasonable expectation of being authentic?

Or were they merely playing the lottery, hoping for the win against all odds?

From their history, he could see either scenario being the truth.

And it could explain the secrecy. This Father Amanuel might have demanded secrecy if they were to take the job. In fact, Leroux was willing to bet the man had never told the professors specifically what it was they were preserving.

Though knowing them, they would have figured it out, which was why they were willing to go along with the demand for secrecy.

"Okay, Dean, we'll look into it."

"Oh, there's one more thing."

Leroux paused. "What?"

"One of my students found something on the Dark Web, where it appears somebody is claiming they know where the Ark is, and is taking deposits to enter a bidding war for the information."

Now that's *interesting. And actionable.*

"Can you send us that information?"

"I already have."

Leroux glanced at Child who nodded, tapping at his keyboard then jerking his chin toward the displays.

"Okay, Dean, we have it, thank you. We'll look into it."

"Thanks."

The call ended and Leroux quickly scanned the posts as they scrolled past, but Child was ahead of him.

"The idiot posted his bank account info!"

Leroux chuckled, shaking his head.

We do love our amateurs.

"Okay, run it."

"Already on it," said Tong, her skills on display as moments later the records appeared of the owner, a numbered company in the Caymans. "I've got access to the account. Looks like a string of ten thousand dollar deposits, most within an hour of each other, then a thousand dollar cash withdrawal from an ATM in New York City, then a bunch more hundred thousand dollar deposits. Whoever owns this account has got some serious dough now."

Leroux paused. "What was the opening balance this morning?"

Tong scrolled back. "Under thirty dollars." She scrolled back some more. "It looks like they get monthly deposits of about three grand, going back for years."

"And suddenly, today, he's got over a million dollars, from over a dozen sources. This guy didn't hit the jackpot, he hit the jackpot that keeps paying."

Child chewed his cheek for a moment. "Sounds like someone with something to sell. Something that without even proof, people are willing to pay a lot for."

Leroux turned to Tong. "That ATM withdrawal—"

"Waaay ahead of you." She tapped a key and leaned back, staring at the display at the front of the room.

And Leroux smiled.

It was Asrat Fida, withdrawing cash, his grinning, wide-eyed face captured by the machine's built-in camera.

We've got you now.

The Oval Office, The White House
Washington, DC

"Leif, good to see you. How's the wife and kids?"

National Clandestine Service Chief Leif Morrison shook President Jacob Starling's hand then took a seat. "They're very well, sir. And your daughter Nancy, how is she?"

"A handful, like all teenage girls."

Morrison chuckled. "I went through it myself, sir. Some days I'm glad it's over, others I'd give anything to have it back."

Starling sat across from him, the last of his staff leaving, closing the door behind them. "Now, what is it that you asked for an emergency meeting, alone?"

Morrison shook his head. "I'm sorry, sir, but this, I hope, is going to turn out to be one of those things that is so stupid in retrospect, that you'll fire me if it ever gets out. But if it isn't, well, it just couldn't wait."

Starling's eyes narrowed as he leaned forward, his elbows on his knees. "You've got my attention."

"Sir, what do you know of the Ark of the Covenant?"

Starling's eyes shot wide. "Okay, I wasn't expecting that. Aliens, yeah, but the Ark?" He shrugged. "I don't know, the usual, I guess. Just what the Bible and Indiana Jones taught me. Why?"

"You've heard me mention professors James Acton and Laura Palmer before?"

Starling nodded. "Of course. They've caused us a lot of headaches over the years."

"Yes, but they've also done a lot of good."

"Which is the only reason I haven't had his passport seized, and asked the Brits to do the same to hers."

Morrison chuckled. "You're a more patient man than I am, Mr. President."

Starling paused. "Wait, are you telling me they've found it?"

"We think there's a possibility. They're in Ethiopia now, on a job we believe to preserve some sort of artifact."

"And you think that artifact is the Ark."

"We have reason to believe it is possible, though it likely is a fake. Our sources indicate they were hired by a Father Amanuel, who works from a church in Ethiopia in an area of the country known to claim to have the Ark. Dozens of churches make the claim, however, which is why we think it's a fake."

"Then why are you here?"

"Because at the same time, somebody on the Dark Web has claimed to know where the Ark is, and is offering that information for sale to the highest bidder. Over a dozen have paid six figures just for a chance at the information."

"Who's making the claim?"

"An American citizen originally from Ethiopia. We have him on camera, along with an Ethiopian citizen, breaking into the professors' house after they left for Ethiopia with the equipment required to build a chamber to control the climate within it."

Starling pursed his lips as he leaned back, folding his arms. "This is very thin, Leif, very thin."

"But what if it's true?"

"So, what if it is? An important piece of history is found."

Morrison shook his head. "I'm sorry, sir, but I think you're missing the point."

Starling smiled slightly. "I've been accused of worse. Enlighten me."

"I mean, sir, what if it is *real*."

Starling stared at him blankly then his eyes flared. "Oooh, you mean…" His jaw dropped slightly. "Well, we can't have *that*."

"No, sir, we can't."

"But how can we know? I mean, let's say it is the actual Ark, which is highly unlikely, how do we know it has the power of God? I mean, I believe in God as much as the next man, but I'm not sure I believe everything I read in the Bible, especially the Old Testament."

"I feel exactly the same, sir, perhaps I'm even more of a skeptic. But if there's even the remotest possibility, we have to do something. Don't we?"

Starling shook his head then rose, pacing in front of his desk. "If the wrong people got their hands on it, and it did have the power of God, the consequences could be devastating. I mean, how do you stop a weapon with the power of God? Nuke it? Would that even work? And even if it did, at what cost?"

"My concern is more what happens if the wrong people simply get their hands on it. What would happen if some Islamist group got it, then destroyed it in public? We could be looking at a holy war. Millions could die."

"What do you recommend?"

"We go in and take it."

"And use it ourselves?"

Morrison shook his head. "I would hope not. Maybe we just stick it in a box then in a warehouse."

Starling paused, staring at him. "Like the movie."

"Like the movie."

Starling scratched at his nose, resuming his pacing. "Leif, this is the most insane thing I think I've ever heard in the office or anywhere, but if there's even the remotest possibility even part of it is true, we could be looking at serious trouble for this nation and its citizens." He stopped and turned to face Morrison. "Leif, do whatever it takes. I want that thing in American hands and no one else's."

Marseilles, France

Alexie Tankov sat with the others from his team of professional art acquirers, their services available to the highest bidder, though that wasn't their only criteria. The collector had to be willing and able to preserve what they acquired.

They weren't destroyers of history, though they didn't mind killing if it became necessary.

He was not the good man his mother thought him to be.

Though he wasn't pure evil like some of his competitors.

Nor were the others, all former Spetsnaz, Russian Special Forces. Highly trained, highly motivated, and well equipped, living the dream between jobs, and keeping their skills honed while on the job.

That was why when the proof was offered up after the hundred thousand was deposited, he spotted the problem right away. "Bring up that invoice, the second one with the generator on it."

His second in command, Utkin, tapped away at his tablet, the large screen they were all watching on mirroring his display.

Could the guy be that stupid?

He held out his hand. "Give it to me."

Utkin handed him the tablet and Tankov zoomed in on the blacked out address at the top of the invoice.

And smiled.

"Gentlemen, we are definitely dealing with an amateur here." He handed the tablet back to Utkin. "Clean that up. Is the person who placed the order who I think it is?"

Utkin worked his magic, and with a few taps and drags, the contrast was adjusted, the weak black marker and the crisp dark of the invoice now clearly different.

Revealing the name of the person who had placed the order.

Laura Palmer.

And the delivery address of Aksum, Ethiopia.

Tankov smiled. "How did I know they'd somehow be involved? Find out where Acton and Palmer are. I'm guessing you can start looking in Aksum. Wherever they are, that's where the Ark is."

Utkin chuckled. "Unbelievable." He frowned. "Do you think the others will figure it out?"

"Probably. If not, they deserve to pay the winning bid."

Utkin pointed at the screen. "You're right. Look at the logged in user count. It's dropping. Looks like they've figured it out."

Tankov shook his head when the number dropped to two. "Us and the seller, I'm guessing." He sighed. "Let the idiot know why he just lost out on what could have been the biggest payday in history. Then find me those professors." He turned to the others. "Start prepping our gear and load the plane. I want to be wheels up by the top of the hour."

Bedford Park, New York City

Fida stared at the screen, his mouth agape, all the users bidding now logged out except one. His heart fluttered as his glorious future, certain only moments ago, crumbled around him.

What's going on?

They had all paid their ten grand without hesitation, then the hundred.

Then it all went bad.

Fast.

His laptop beeped with a message from the final logged in user, his shoulders slumping as the display showed them logging out a moment later. He opened the message and bit his finger to stop himself from crying out in anger and anguish.

When you redact something, make sure the marker is a little darker. Better luck next time.

He grabbed the printouts of the invoices, then held them up to the light over his booth. And cursed, Laura Palmer's name clearly legible on one of them, along with the delivery address. He threw the papers against the window then slammed his fists on the table repeatedly as a piteous rage overwhelmed him.

"Sir!"

His clenched fists hovered over the table and his head spun toward the intruding voice, a young waitress standing nearby, putting on a brave face of authority, but clearly terrified at what she might be about to encounter.

He was aghast.

"I-I'm sorry. I'm leaving." He quickly gathered everything, jammed it in his backpack, then rushed from the diner, but not before tossing several twenties on the table.

He rushed down the street, putting some distance between himself and the embarrassing situation he had created, praying no one had called the police. He had screwed up. Big. His payday would never come, all because he hadn't properly blacked out the names. He had printed them out rather than edit them electronically, because he had been scared that the original data might be just hidden, and someone in the know might be able to remove his electronic redacts.

He had been a fool.

He froze in mid-stride, causing those behind him to curse at him as he became a stone in the river of humanity.

I have the deposits!

He grabbed his phone, launching the banking app that would let him see his balance.

And smiled.

Well over a million dollars.

It was more than enough for him to escape this life of poverty. If he was smart about it, he could have a little fun, then set himself up for life.

A food truck!

It had always been his dream, at least since he had become acquainted with life in America. What could be better than being outdoors, cooking delicious food, interacting with happy customers, and making money?

It was what he had always wanted.

Independence.

Pride in his work.

He resumed walking, checking the balance once again.

And became woozy, stumbling sideways and almost collapsing before his outstretched hand found the roof of a parked car. He steadied himself, then stared at the phone again.

Account balance: $0.00.

His laptop beeped in his bag and he rushed to a nearby bench, removing it and flipping open the top, his TOR browser still logged in to the Dark Web auction site. There was a new user logged in, and a message. He selected it and tapped his thumb twice to open it.

If you ever want to see your money again, contact us. Now.

He shook as he stared at the phone number at the end of the message. Whoever this was had the power to empty an account only he was supposed to have access to. That meant they were powerful. Dangerous. He should just walk away. Toss the laptop, his phone, everything, and disappear. These were dangerous people he was dealing with, and most likely it was someone who wanted their money back.

Or worse.

But if they just wanted their money back, then why take it all? And why bother contacting him?

Something more was going on here.

And his future dreams were at stake.

He dialed the number.

Operations Center 3, CIA Headquarters

Langley, Virginia

"It's him."

Leroux nodded at Tong as he adjusted his headset. The auctioneer had called quickly, their message only posted minutes ago after they had drained the account. Their new orders, direct from the President, were to acquire the Ark at all costs, and this man might be the key to that, for at the moment, the professors were lost to them in a huge country with few ways to locate anyone.

This call was critical.

"To whom am I speaking?"

The man wasn't having any of that, though the voice stress analyzer on the display was indicating fear and nervousness. "To whom am *I* speaking?"

"I'm the man who has your money, and I'm the only one who can give it back."

"That money is mine! I earned it!"

The display indicated the man indeed thought that was true. "Did you, now? From what I can tell, your little auction has failed. You have no bidders. Probably because you didn't redact your documents properly. Very foolish. Next time use your computer to redact them, then make sure you flatten the layers. It will remove the original data."

"Why are you telling me this?"

"Because you are clearly an amateur, and I don't think you'll ever have need of the knowledge in the future."

"What do you mean?"

"I have a feeling you stumbled upon something and decided to try and make a little money."

Child snapped his fingers and pointed at the screen. A map was displayed, a red dot pulsating in the center, their subject in Bedford Park, New York City.

Leroux muted his mike. "Roll units to that location, but have them hold back. And see if you can get him on camera." He reactivated his mike. "Am I right?"

There was a hesitation, but he finally replied. "Yes."

The trace data appeared on the screen, including the name the phone was registered to, reconfirming just how much of an amateur the man was.

Use a burner phone if you're going to commit a crime.

But it did reconfirm one thing. It was Asrat Fida, one of their two subjects that had broken into the professors' house.

"So, Mr. Fida, I need to ask you a few questions."

191

The stress indicator skyrocketed. "H-how do you know my name?"

"I know everything about you. Your name, your address, your phone number. That you were born in Ethiopia, you immigrated to the United States over ten years ago, you got your citizenship three years ago. I know everything. *Almost* everything. What I don't know is why you were in Professor Acton's house. But I think I know that now, too. You were looking for those invoices. The real question is how did you know to look for them? Obviously, you were told there was something to find there, and you were told to make it look like no one had searched the house. So, I guess I know the answer to that question as well." He paused. "What I really want to know, Mr. Fida, is who are you working for?"

"I-I can't say." If the stress analyzer could indicate an impending heart attack, the readings now shown were surely it. "I-I'm going to hang up now."

"Hang up, Mr. Fida, and you'll never see your money again."

"You-you mean you'll give it back to me?"

Got you now!

"Have you hurt anybody?"

"No."

"Have you killed anybody?"

"Of course not!"

"Did you steal the money?"

"Umm, no, I don't think so."

"So, right now, all you're guilty of is breaking and entering."

"I suppose so."

"Then I don't see any reason why I can't give you your money back. In fact, how about I give you ten grand back right now."

"You'd do that?"

"Sure. As a gesture of good faith."

He muted his mike. "Transfer ten back. This guy's so blinded by the money, I have a feeling we're going to get everything we want out of him without having to bring him in."

"The money's there," said Tong.

He unmuted. "Can you check your balance?"

"Yes."

"Do it."

"Okay."

Child snapped his fingers, pointing at the display, and Leroux smiled, a security camera showing Fida sitting on a bench, a laptop on his knees, a phone in his hand.

Fida smiled.

"When can I get the rest?"

"When you answer all my questions. Truthfully. If I think for even one second that you're lying to me, I take it all back and buy myself a boat."

Snickers filled the room.

"Answer honestly, and you'll be rewarded. Okay?"

"Okay."

"Your name is Asrat Fida."

"Yes."

"Why were you in professors Acton and Palmer's house?"

"To look for, umm, evidence."

"Evidence of what?"

"Of whether they told anyone what they were doing."

"And did you find any?"

"No."

"And what is it they're doing?"

"They're, umm, going to help preserve something."

"Very good. You've earned another ten grand." He motioned to Tong who tapped a few keys then nodded. "Check your phone."

He watched as Fida swiped his phone, a grin appearing. "Thank you!"

"Units are in position," whispered Child.

Leroux acknowledged him with a nod. "Now, what is it they're trying to preserve?"

"Umm..."

Fida was looking about, clearly unsure of what to do.

"Tell me, or I take the money back."

"It's the Ark of the Covenant!" came the hasty reply, money clearly the most important motivator in Fida's life.

Leroux closed his eyes for a moment, muting his mike, as the room exploded in murmured shock at the confirmation. He held up a hand, silencing them, then unmuted. "And how are the professors involved?"

"They've been hired by the Keeper to preserve the Ark. Apparently, it's in danger of falling apart."

"The Keeper?"

"He's the man responsible for preserving the Ark."

"And what's his name?"

"Father Amanuel."

"And what church is he at?"

"He serves several, I think. I'm not really sure exactly which ones. I've been gone for so long."

So far, everything Fida had told them matched with what they already knew. But now came the real questions, the ones they had no answers for.

That meant a little more grease had to be provided.

"I think you've earned another ten grand."

Tong gave the thumbs up and Fida checked his phone then smiled.

"Now, who do you work for?"

Fida said nothing, instead looking over both shoulders. "Umm, I, umm, can't say."

"You just lost ten grand."

"Wait! Okay, I'll tell you. It doesn't matter anyway. Too many people know now. It's all over."

Leroux wanted to ask him why, but he had more important questions that needed to be answered and didn't want to stop the man from spilling his greedy guts.

"I'm with the Sons of Tamrin."

"And who are they?"

"We're tasked to make sure the priests, the Keepers, keep their word."

"Which is?"

"To never reveal the existence of the Ark to anyone."

"And if they don't keep their word?"

"Then we're supposed to try and preserve the secret for them, or…"

"Or?"

"Or destroy the Ark before it's exposed to the world."

Leroux pursed his lips, not liking where this was going. "You said it's too late. What did you mean?"

"The professors know, or if they don't by now, they'll know soon. Once they see the Ark, my order can't risk them telling anyone, especially because they're so well respected. People might believe them."

"What does your order have planned?"

"We're going to kill them as soon as they've completed their task."

Leroux shook his head, suppressing a curse, though not surprised. "Why not kill them before?"

"Because the Ark needs to be preserved. If we kill the professors now, then someone else will be hired to do the job. They need to complete their task, then we'll kill them to preserve the secret."

"But don't a lot of people know now? You tried to sell its location on the web to the highest bidder."

"I-I just wanted to make some money. I figured between the priests and the order, the Ark would be safe, and if it wasn't, then the order would destroy it and my job here would be done, and I could get out of this damned life."

And now the question he had a feeling he wasn't going to get an answer to. "Where is the Ark, exactly?"

"I don't really know. They move it around. And I've been gone for over ten years."

Exactly as I thought.

"Who would know?"

"Senior members of the order should."

"Like Dawit Ganno?"

He watched Fida's jaw drop. "You know about him?"

"Remember, I know everything. Would Ganno know?"

"Y-yes. He should."

"Very well. Thank you for your time."

Leroux ended the call. "Pull back the money, send the team in."

Tong grinned. "You're cold."

"Threaten to kill Americans, and I always am."

They all watched as the team rushed in, arresting Fida swiftly and without incident.

"Find me Ganno. I'm going to brief the Chief."

Unknown Location

South of Aksum, Ethiopia

"Well, our faces didn't melt, so that's a good sign."

Laura gave Acton a look. "We're not Nazis."

"Was that the rule?"

Laura shrugged. "I don't exactly get my history lessons from Indiana Jones movies."

Acton gave her a toothy grin. "When we get home, we are sooo doing an Indy marathon."

"I'll be doing my hair."

"Sometimes I wonder why I ever married you."

"Mind-blowing sex?"

Acton smiled. "Oh yeah."

Father Amanuel returned and their conversation was halted, Acton left to wonder if the old man had heard the last part.

"Have you decided?"

Laura nodded. "We have. Whether this is real or not is irrelevant. You've hired us to do a job, and we intend to do it."

"How long do you need?"

"Not much, if we have help with the physical side of things."

"Are six men enough?"

"Hopefully." Laura pointed toward the stairs. "The first thing we'll get them working on is positioning the generator. Do you have a place in mind? It needs to be well ventilated, preferably outside, no more than a hundred feet from where we're standing."

"I do."

"Okay, we'll get them to move the generator into position, then have them bring the rest of the equipment into here to assemble. Once it's set up, we just move the Ark into position, close it up, turn on the system, and we're good to go."

Amanuel smiled. "Excellent. We should work quickly, before they discover your presence here."

"Who are 'they?'" asked Acton.

"It doesn't matter. But we must work quickly."

Acton frowned. "That's at least the second time you've mentioned another party. I think we have the right to know who you're talking about."

Amanuel regarded him for a moment then sighed. "Fine. They are called the Sons of Tamrin. They were created at the same time our order was, by King Menelik. They think we don't know about them, but over the millennia we became aware."

"And their purpose?"

"To act as a backup, I suppose. They take action if we fail."

Laura's eyes narrowed. "Fail?"

"Reveal the secret to someone, or if someone discovers the Ark, despite our best efforts."

Acton pursed his lips, not liking what he was hearing. "And if you fail, what do they do?"

"They will do whatever it takes to preserve the secret."

"Such as?"

"They won't hesitate to kill you if they discover you are here. They will not risk you telling anyone that the Ark exists."

Acton tensed, his fists clenching. "And should they find out we were here after the fact?"

Amanuel stared at the floor. "It's best they don't."

Acton's jaw squared as he shook his head. "And you didn't think to tell us this before we agreed to take the job?"

Amanuel looked at him. "Would you have said yes?"

"Absolutely not!"

The old man regarded him for a moment, then shook his head. "I don't believe you. I think your decision was made the moment you realized it was the Ark, and there would be no changing your mind, no matter what I said."

Acton muttered a curse, the man probably right. He headed for the stairs. "Let's get going. I want to be out of here before nightfall."

Director Morrison's Office, CIA Headquarters
Langley, Virginia

"Can you find this Ganno?"

Leroux nodded at his boss. "Yes, sir. We already have. He's on a flight about to land in an hour, then he's booked on a second flight for Aksum in northern Ethiopia. The same area that Father Amanuel is from."

Morrison chewed his cheek. "Can you track him?"

"We have an asset already on the ground. He's a local we've used before. We've also retasked a satellite, and have three drones assigned to cover the area. We should be able to follow him, hopefully straight to the professors."

Morrison shook his head, leaning back in his chair. "Did you ever think the CIA, under orders from the President himself, would be directing an operation to recover the Ark of the Covenant?"

Leroux grunted. "I can honestly say it never would have occurred to me in a million years. Then again, we've dealt with some weird things with these professors."

Morrison leaned forward, dropping his elbows onto his desk. "Yeah, but wrath of God type stuff?"

"You think it's real?"

Morrison shrugged. "I don't know. I don't *think* so. I mean, I'm as religious as the next guy, I guess, though it's been a long time since I've seen the inside of a church. My wife is more the devout one than I am. And beyond Sunday school, I've never read the Bible. But I believe in God. If you don't, what's the damned purpose for being on this ball of rock hurtling through space if in the end you're just dust." He sighed, staring at his underling. "Chris, I don't know what to think. All I know is that if there's the remotest possibility, we can't let that thing fall into the wrong hands. It could mean the end of everything."

Leroux stared at him. "Sir?"

"Nuclear war."

"Do you think it could come to that?"

"If it's real, and gives an army that possesses it the power of God, then yes. It might be the only way to stop them."

"But surely God wouldn't let it be used for evil purposes."

Morrison regarded him. "Chris, have you ever wondered, if we're all worshipping the same God, whose side is He on? What if we're not the good guys after all?"

Leroux shuddered. "I'm not sure I want to think about the possibility."

"Exactly. So, let's just get this damned thing, throw it in a cold dark corner somewhere, and forget about it."

"Good idea." Leroux rose. "Oh, and to that end, we're going to need boots on the ground."

"Already in the works."

Somewhere over the Arabian Sea

"Listen, fartknocker, if it wasn't for me, you never would have met Vanessa."

Command Sergeant Major Burt "Big Dog" Dawson smiled, along with the rest of Bravo Team, all members of 1st Special Forces Operational Detachment–Delta, commonly known as the Delta Force, the nation's most elite of soldiers, and from any outside observer, its most dysfunctional. Between missions. On the job, they were deadly and efficient. Off the job, they were the best of friends, which meant it was usually open season on each other.

Like today, in the back of a C-130J Super Hercules.

The impossibly muscled Sergeant Leon "Atlas" James stared at the diminutive in comparison Sergeant Carl "Niner" Sung. "What makes you figure that?"

"I introduced you! Don't you remember how you met her?"

"I remember, but I think I remember something completely different than you."

Niner shook his head, looking at the others. "You guys remember, don't you?"

Heads shook, and Sergeant Will "Spock" Lightman's eyebrow cocked. "I think you're on your own with this one, buddy."

"Sure, abandon me in my time of need." He jabbed a finger at Atlas. "She never told you, did she?"

Atlas eyed him. "Told me what?"

"Why she went up to you at the bar that night?"

Dawson could tell Atlas was either waiting for a punchline or getting ready for some unwanted knowledge to drop. Either would be fun.

"I have no idea what you're talking about."

Niner paused. "Huh. I wonder why she wouldn't tell you?"

"Tell me what?"

"Maybe I shouldn't say. When we get back, I'll get her to clear it. Maybe she thinks you'll get jealous."

Atlas inflated his massive chest. "I don't get jealous."

"Bullshit. One 'dayum' from a guy and you're having words."

"That's true, and I wish you would stop saying that every time you see her."

Niner grinned. "I know I should, but dayum, that girl's hot."

Atlas turned to Dawson. "Permission to split this mother like a wishbone, Sergeant Major?"

Dawson chuckled. "I might need him later. Feel free to tenderize him a bit."

Atlas grinned and Niner bolted, grabbing Sergeant Gerry "Jimmy Olsen" Hudson and placing him between them.

"Okay, fine, do you want to know what happened that night?"

"Tell me now, or I might disobey an order."

"Well, that night, you pointed her out and said 'dayum, she's fine.'"

"I said no such thing."

The entire plane disagreed.

"So, being the good friend that I am, I went to the bathroom, then on my way back, I went to her table and pointed at you and told her you wanted me to ask her if she was wearing any panties."

"What?" Atlas appeared horrified. "I'm going to kill you!"

Niner stepped back, waving his hands. "No, no, let me finish. So, she pointed at you and said something like, 'What, the big guy with the too-tight shirt?'"

Snickers.

"And I said, 'No, not him, he's a sweetie. And single. I'm talking about the guy to his right.'"

Atlas' eyes narrowed. "Wait, wasn't Spock sitting to my right that night?"

Spock's jaw dropped. "You bastard! That's why she was giving me the evil eye all night!"

Niner grinned. "Anyway, I told her you'd really like to meet her but was a shy guy despite your ridiculous biceps, and she came over a few minutes later."

Atlas eyed him, his lips thrust out. "I don't believe you."

"Believe it."

Spock looked at Atlas. "She *did* give me the stink-eye all night. There had to be a reason."

Atlas sighed. "The sad thing is that every word he just said, I believe him completely capable of. I mean, what kind of guy goes up to a girl and asks her if she's wearing panties."

"Hey, I didn't. I said Spock wanted to know."

"But you still asked her!"

"Ahh, she knew I was just trying to get you two together."

Spock threw an MRE at him. "Bullshit, otherwise there wouldn't have been the dirty looks."

Niner shrugged. "Maybe she just doesn't like you."

"We get along fine now."

Niner cocked his head to the side. "Do you? I mean, really, do you?"

Dawson's comm squawked in his ear. "Zero-One, Control Actual. Do you copy?"

He rose and headed for the rear of the plane, the Colonel contacting him unusual. "Yes, sir, I copy."

"Are you alone?"

"Alone as I'm going to be, sir."

"Good. I've got a new mission for you, details are being sent to your secure phone. And you're not going to believe it."

"I've learned to mask my surprise, sir."

Colonel Thomas Clancy, the Unit's Commanding Officer, chuckled. "Even you're going to be surprised at this one."

Now Dawson's curiosity was piqued. "Hit me, sir."

"You're going after the Ark of the Covenant."

Dawson's eyes shot wide.

Then narrowed.

"Is it April First?"

"No joke, Sergeant Major. Our archaeology friends may have found it, and apparently a shitstorm of questionable collectors is about to rain down on them. The President himself has ordered us to get there first, secure the item, then get it and the professors out of harm's way. Should you be unable to secure the item, you're to destroy it."

Dawson shook his head, thinking of the past encounters he had enjoyed with the professors, including their first encounter, where he had tried to kill James Acton. He had been provided false intel by a corrupt president who had claimed the man and his students were domestic terrorists who had killed US Army personnel and stolen a top secret DARPA project.

It had all been bullshit, but by the time they discovered their orders were illegal, it was too late.

Too many innocents were dead, including some of his own men.

In the ensuing years, he and his men had tried to make up for their crimes, despite being cleared of any fault. He considered Acton and his wife Laura friends, friends he and the others wouldn't hesitate to put their lives on the line for, just as these two civilians had done for them.

But rescuing them from terrorists, cults, gangs, or whatnot, didn't hold a candle to this.

Yet it had to be bullshit.

"The Ark of the Covenant. That big golden box from Raiders."

"One and the same."

Dawson grunted. "This has to be a joke, right? I mean, it's not real, right?"

"No idea, Sergeant Major, and I don't care. The powers that be think there's a possibility it could be real, and even if it isn't, it could spark reprisals should it fall into the wrong hands and be used as a pawn in a holy war."

Dawson's head bobbed. Now *that* he could see. Grab it, secure it, and lives could be saved, even if it was merely a Hollywood prop. "Okay, sir, we'll grab it. The boys are going to get a kick out of this."

"Need to know, Sergeant Major, and they don't need to know. As far as they're concerned, they're going in to recover an item the professors have discovered, and are rescuing their old friends."

"I trust my men, sir."

"As do I, Sergeant Major, but I don't want any hesitation based on religious beliefs. Remember, if you can't secure it, you must destroy it. If it comes to that, it's best they don't know what they're blowing up."

Dawson frowned. He trusted his men with his life, but the Colonel was right. Even he was somewhat uncomfortable with the idea. Though he couldn't believe it was the real Ark, even if there was the slightest chance it was, blowing it up seemed like a horrible idea, and he was certain others on the team would have reservations as well. "We'll just have to make sure it doesn't come to that."

"Let's hope."

Dawson tensed as a thought occurred to him. "Sir, who has it now?"

"It's all in the package I sent you, but we believe it's a priest, probably a group of priests."

Dawson pursed his lips. "And should they object to us taking the Ark?"

"Use non-lethal force if possible, but we need that Ark in safe hands. The shitstorm that is coming down on them is something the priests are not going to be able to handle. Every well-financed criminal organization is likely already en route. We're just hoping you get there first."

"Copy that, sir, I'll brief the men. We'll get the job done."

"I know you will, Sergeant Major. Control, out."

Dawson quickly scanned the encrypted file Clancy had sent him, shaking his head with every paragraph, before briefing the team, giving them all the specifics he could beyond what the object was.

Niner eyed him. "What is it you're not telling us?" He snapped his fingers. "It's the item. You didn't say what it was we're supposed to be recovering."

"Need to know, Sergeant."

Atlas rolled his eyes. "Ugh, please tell me it's not another one of those damned crystal skulls. Those things give me the creeps." He shivered. "And the shivers."

Niner grabbed his pack, making a show of searching it. "Vanessa had me bring your teddy bear, just in case you were having nightmares. It's in here somewhere. Give me a sec."

The team roared with laughter at Atlas' expense, one-liners zinging back and forth before Dawson put up a hand, cutting them off.

"Get some rack time, ladies, we're going to be in the thick of it sooner than you know." He rose to head for the cockpit, but stopped for one last jab. "And Atlas, since Niner lost your teddy bear, I suggest you snuggle with him. He's about the right size."

Atlas grinned as the others laughed. "Come over here, little one, Papa likes to spoon."

Aksum, Ethiopia

There are a lot of white boys here today.

Hassen Tesfay sat in his truck, parked outside the small airport in Aksum, an airport not known for tourists, and certainly not groups of four to ten men arriving together on chartered planes and transports.

Something was up, and he had no doubt it had everything to do with the contract he was now on. His handler had never told him who he was working for when hiring him, though he was certain it was the American government, most likely the CIA.

He didn't care. It was money. Good money in a place like this. It fed his wife and children—three sons and two daughters—as well as his mother.

But the work was dangerous. Extremely dangerous in a country like Ethiopia. Here people would kill you for your shoes or your phone, though he had heard the same was true in America.

Now *there* was the dream. He hoped eventually he'd be able to ask his handler to move him and his family there once he had proven himself useful. The possibility had been suggested when he was recruited, but nothing had been mentioned since, and he was afraid to bring it up lest his handler drop him.

He was stuck between keeping the job that could get him killed, or asking for the implied promise to be fulfilled, and risking losing the job that kept his family alive. And if he were found out? They would all be dead for certain.

And that was why he had never told his wife what he did, how he kept them fed. If she told the wrong person, it would all be over.

He watched a little girl walk by, one hand held by her mother, the other occupied by a candy hardened around a small stick, the little girl licking at it furiously.

He smiled, the precious thing reminding him of his youngest daughter.

He snapped some more photos of another set of new arrivals, then squinted as his primary target strolled into the sunlight, a group of men climbing out of their car and embracing him as if he had been away on a long journey.

Yet Ganno had only been gone for a few days.

Apparently, these men were rarely separated.

They climbed into their car, Ganno getting the prized passenger seat, then pulled into traffic. Tesfay started his engine, cranked the wheel, and was about to hit the gas when a pickup truck skidded to a halt, cutting him off. A man leaned out the window and wagged a finger at him, then produced an AK-47. Tesfay shoved his door open and rolled out onto the pavement, covering his head, as the assault rifle opened fire, sending the crowds screaming and fleeing in all directions.

Then it stopped, his assailants roaring away in a cloud of dust. He pushed to his feet, assessing himself for damage, then checked to see if anyone else had been hurt.

None.

Except his poor truck.

Steam hissed from the engine compartment, and as he approached, he cursed at the sight, the couple dozen rounds emptied into the hood having done their job. He climbed back inside and activated his comm as he collected his things.

"Control, this is Whiskey-Alpha-Four. I think I've been made, over."

"What makes you think that?"

"Umm, the thirty rounds in my engine block."

Control chuckled. "Yeah, that might suggest you've been noticed. Did you ID the car?"

"Yeah, it's a white Toyota sedan traveling south from my current position. He's probably only a couple of hundred meters from here."

"Stand by." There was a pause, though only for a moment. "Okay, we've got him for now. Get another vehicle and we'll guide you in."

"Roger that. I'm going to upload some photos to you. There are a lotta white boys here today. Tough guys, if you know what I mean."

"Mercenaries?"

"They look the type. Some Middle Eastern looking gentlemen as well that match the profile. I'm guessing whatever is going on is attracting some outside interest."

"Any indication they're following our target?"

"Negative, but maybe they've got eyes in the sky too?"

"Or they're just pre-positioning, awaiting intel. They probably know our professors are already there, just not where."

"Copy that." He spotted a group of soldiers rolling up on his position. "Control, I'm drawing attention. I'm going to find a secure location then upload those photos. Whiskey-Alpha-Four, out."

One big break is all I need.

But if big breaks were easy to come by, everyone would be getting them. Captain Mussa had joined the military as an escape from the never-ending cycle of poverty his family had been trapped in for generations, and to take advantage of an uncle who had made out like a bandit after the civil war and was able to secure his nephew a position as an officer.

The gateway to riches.

Or so he had been told.

The lion's share of any bribe went to the highest officers, and as he climbed through the ranks, his share kept improving. But the real money was in discovering some score where those caught were so desperate, they offered princely sums for their freedom.

The big break that could change a life forever.

He was still waiting for his.

Gunfire in the distance had him standing upright in his technical, his sergeant firing up the engine.

"Sounds like someone just emptied an AK into someone."

Mussa agreed. "Sounds like it's coming from the airport. Could be trouble. Let's roll, see what we find."

It only took a couple of minutes to arrive on the scene, the only evidence of any wrongdoing the smoking engine of a truck, the apparent victim of the AK, his fellow countrymen already going about their daily business, whatever had happened forgotten.

And it didn't surprise him.

Gunfire was simply a way of life in Ethiopia. It wasn't as bad as it had been in the past, but to call this a peaceful country would mean one was a liar or simply ignorant. He was neither. This was probably some traffic dispute gone wrong, or a message being sent to the owner. Either way, there would be no financial gain today.

Heavy gunfire erupted farther down the street and he rose in his seat to investigate. Two groups of heavily armed men were firing on each other, both hidden behind sets of vehicles, both definitely not local.

That meant foreign money.

If they survived the day.

"Call in the rest of the unit. This is going to get ugly."

Operations Center 3, CIA Headquarters

Langley, Virginia

"Any indication where he's heading?"

Tong shook her head. "Just the general direction, which is toward the church M. Giasson identified as that of Father Amanuel."

Leroux stepped closer to the displays curving across the front of the operations center, his hands on his hips as he monitored the drone footage. "Okay, get that church's location to Delta along with any intel we have on it. Pictures of the area, etcetera. I want them going in with as much intel as we can give them."

Child blasted some air through his lips. "We don't even know if that's where he's going. We came up with nada on Father Amanuel's arrival and the professors, so we have no idea if they're actually there."

Leroux glanced at him. "It's an educated guess. They're at least in the area, so if we can put our people close to where they need to be, they can act quickly when we know for sure." He stared at the footage, telling them nothing useful. They needed to know where the Ark was hidden. Right now, Ganno was probably heading for the vicinity, but that just meant more hostiles Delta might have to deal with. And Tesfay had reported that additional foreign elements were arriving in the area already, which meant more guns, which meant more risk to their people.

"We need better intel. Get someone in a room with Mr. Fida. He must have a contact number. Maybe it's something we can ping and triangulate like a satphone."

Tong nodded. "I'm on it."

He turned to Child. "What about those photos Tesfay sent us? Any luck IDing the people?"

Child shook his head. "We haven't received them yet."

"What? Do we have a drone still there?"

"Yes, sir."

"Show me his last known position."

Child brought up the footage, the drone repositioning over Aksum before focusing on the road in front of the airport.

"Holy shit!"

Aksum, Ethiopia

Tesfay ducked as gunfire erupted all around him. His head swiveled, searching for shelter, but finding none that wasn't already teeming with terrified shoppers, and he wasn't willing to push one of them out of the way to save his own skin.

He was better than that.

And it would probably get him killed.

Two groups of the new arrivals were battling it out. Who, he wasn't sure, but they were well armed with plenty of ammo. Better equipped than the Ethiopian regulars that had rolled up on the situation, probably initially to investigate the attack on his truck.

There was a pause in the shooting, one of those unusual moments where everyone ran out of ammo at the same time, or were all taking cover from each other.

Whatever the cause, it gave him a moment of clarity from his position, now prone in the dirt.

A little girl was crying.

He turned to find her, then cursed when he saw the child from earlier, her candy still gripped in her hand, but her mother nowhere in sight, as she stood in the middle of the road, in the middle of the three battling parties. He pushed to his feet and rushed toward her, holding his hands over his head as best he could while at a crouch, hoping the shooters would recognize his actions as stupidity rather than hostility.

And all hell broke loose once again, the brief reprieve over.

He dropped to his knees, pleading for the little girl to come toward him, but she stood frozen in place, tears staining her cheeks while her mouth continued to work the candy between gasped cries.

Please, God, protect us both.

He rushed forward and scooped her up, then spun around, racing for the cover of the vehicles lining the road. Something hit him in the shoulder and he cried out, dropping to a knee, his bag containing all his equipment falling to the ground. He reached for it, but bullets tore into the pavement only feet away.

Save the girl, idiot.

He struggled to his feet then stumbled the last few paces, dropping between two cars.

But it wasn't safe, stray bullets tearing into the metal and tires. He fumbled forward, the girl in one arm, his other aching from the hit he had taken, then spotted an alleyway. On adrenaline alone, he rose and sprinted for the shelter it would provide, the darkness swallowing him up, the deafening rattle of the weapons immediately muted. He put the girl down then pointed at her. "You stay here, okay?"

She nodded, the candy back in her mouth, the flow of tears easing.

He checked his shoulder to find a hole through it, a matching one on his back. A through-and-through.

Thank God for small miracles.

He tore off his sleeve and tied a tourniquet over the wound using his teeth, good hand, and a lot of painful gasps.

He'd live.

Now for the really stupid part.

He needed his bag. It had his weapon, but more importantly, it had his camera, and all the critical intel his handlers were waiting for. He headed back for the street and the gunfire, then assessed the situation from relative safety. He could see his bag, too close to the middle of the road for his liking, though only paces from the vehicles that could provide him with some cover.

To his right was a group he recognized from earlier, three Middle Eastern-looking men hiding behind an SUV, their number half of what they had arrived with. To his left was another group he recognized as well, all white but tanned, their numbers equally diminished.

Then there was the military, farther still to his left, pouring lead on both the warring parties, a few of their number bleeding on the road.

It was a Mexican standoff where no one seemed to care if they survived.

What is it that's so important you don't care if you die?

His handler hadn't told him what this was all about, or at least the truth about what it was about. As far as he had been told, this was about recovering two professors, an American and a Brit, who were in trouble.

But mercenary groups from around the world didn't show up to rescue professors when American Special Forces were already on the job.

No, something else was going on here. These men were motivated by money, and the amount had to be significant for them to be willing to die for a chance at it.

He rushed from the safety of the alley and dove between the two cars he had used as cover earlier. He crawled to the edge of their tires and peered out at the gun battle still raging. He reached for the bag, stretching as far as he could, but came up short by only an arm's length.

He closed his eyes, drew a deep breath, and said a silent prayer.

Then surged forward, grabbing the bag, then dragging it back toward the cars.

Someone noticed, the ground erupting beside him.

He rolled sideways, his back hitting the tire of one of the cars, blocking his retreat, then closed his eyes as the wall of lead reached him.

Then suddenly stopped.

He opened one eye to see the last of the Middle Eastern men eliminated, the white men now battling the military exclusively, both groups to his left. He leaped to his feet and returned to the alley, gripping his bag. He peered into the darkness to see the little girl still standing there, concentrating on her candy, then grabbed his camera and began uploading the photos using his satphone before someone managed to succeed in their attempts to kill him today.

The guns fell silent, somebody finally victorious, and he was willing to bet it was the military. He peered out from his cover, confirming his suspicions, the soldiers now moving in on their opponents' positions.

Something tugged on his pant leg.

He looked down to see the little girl standing there, her candy finished, her arms stretched upward. He picked her up and she wrapped her arms around his neck, resting her head on his shoulder.

"How about we find your mommy, okay?"

"Okay."

Mussa stood over the final remaining hostile, a white man with a dark tan, now lying on the ground, disarmed, his leg oozing blood as his comrades lay either dead or dying around him.

"What was this about?"

The man glared at him. "I'm not telling you anything."

Mussa drove the heel of his boot into the man's wound and he cried out in agony as all color drained from his face. "Want to talk now? I've got all day." He eased up on the pressure, relief washing over his prisoner's face.

"Fine, dammit, I'll tell you. But you've got to let me go."

Mussa shook his head. "You're in no position to negotiate."

"When you hear what I have to say, you'll change your mind." The man beckoned him closer. Mussa glanced about, his men covering the area, all but his sergeant not within earshot.

"What?"

"It's worth tens of millions to whoever finds it first."

Mussa's heart hammered as he realized this could be the break he had been waiting for all these years. "What is it?"

"Do I have your word?"

He nodded. And why not, it wasn't as if he had to keep it.

"It's the Ark."

His eyes narrowed, disappointed. "The what?"

"The Ark of the Covenant. You know, like in the Bible."

"What about it?"

"Somebody found it."

Mussa thought for a moment, trying to think of what the man might be talking about. He had never read the Bible, though considered himself Christian like most in Ethiopia. Then it dawned on him what the man meant, and it sent a surge of excitement through his body. "You mean the Ark of Zion? The Tabota Seyen? That which contains the word of God?"

The man shrugged. "Sure."

"Where is it?"

"I don't know."

Mussa pressed a little harder and the man gasped.

"I'm telling the truth, dammit! It's south of here, that's all I know."

"That hardly helps me."

"Just follow the others like my team. God knows there's enough here that someone has to figure it out."

He placed two bullets in the man's chest.

"Why'd you do that?" asked his sergeant.

"If he tells anyone else, we'll have to share it with more people."

His sergeant chuckled. "I like the way you think. But where are we going to find it?"

"We'll head south, like he said. There are some churches there I know claim they have the Ark. Let's get in the area, look for white people with guns." He surveyed the scene, including his surviving men. "We're going to need more firepower. Gather who you can trust, but tell them nothing. This is our big payday, my friend, and I don't want to risk losing it for the lack of guns."

Unknown Location

South of Aksum, Ethiopia

Acton stood back and surveyed their work. Today, he was just muscle, like the other men. This was Laura's show, and she had them all working like a well-oiled machine. The generator was in place and operational, and the base of their climate controlled portable preservation chamber was ready.

Laura stepped back, pointing at the Ark. "Okay, we need to move the Ark into position."

Father Amanuel stepped forward from his perch in the corner. "That's how it broke."

Laura frowned, examining the two poles, one broken near the middle. "Okay, we're going to have to temporarily replace them. The rings they go through appear to be solid gold and in good condition, so we should be able to use them to move it. Once it's inside the unit, we'll put the original poles back, seal it up, then you'll probably never need to carry it by them again."

Amanuel frowned. "I don't think we have anything that we can use to replace them."

Acton scratched his chin as he puzzled out the problem. "What about the fakes? Can you get the poles from them?"

Amanuel smiled. "Yes." He barked an order and two of the young men sprinted from the room.

"How long?"

"An hour. We should eat while we can."

Acton rubbed his stomach. "Good. I'm starving."

Amanuel issued some more orders, and within minutes food was brought to them in generous quantities. The workers huddled in one corner, eating in silence, while Acton and Laura sat on the floor, cross-legged, with Amanuel.

"So, Father, tell me. Your group was created by Menelik about three thousand years ago?"

"Yes."

"So, they were Jewish, then? Rabbis, not priests?"

"Yes."

"Then why do you keep it hidden because of a prophecy from Jesus?"

Amanuel took a drink of water. "We converted, as did most of the country, and with that came new interpretations of our then thousand-year-old mandate."

"And these others you spoke of, are they Christian too?"

"Yes."

"And do they believe in the prophecy as well?"

"Of course. Remember, nothing really changed. We've always worshipped the same God, experienced the same history. What Menelik asked of us wasn't negated by the prophecy, it merely was reinforced by it. Menelik knew that the Ark must be hidden, he just didn't know the real reason why. Jesus revealed that."

Acton swallowed something delicious. "What will you do if the Ark is found and the world finds out? With the way things are today, there's no way you'll be able to put the genie back in the bottle. There'd be photos and video all over the Internet. It would never be forgotten, which means the prophecy could never be fulfilled."

Amanuel smiled slightly. "Perhaps, though I'm sure God would find a way."

"I hope you're right," said Laura. "The way the world is today, I doubt we'll get a second chance if it takes another hundred years, let alone three thousand."

Amanuel regarded her. "Do you fear for the future, Professor?"

She nodded. "History is my specialty, and every great empire throughout time has fallen, usually when it becomes successful enough to attract those who would take, rather than contribute. Western civilization is at that point now."

Acton agreed. "We're so far ahead of most of the rest of the world, that everyone wants to be inside our borders, and too often for the wrong reasons. It's one thing to come, work hard, and become one with our ways, it's a completely different thing to come and expect to be taken care of, then fight our ways. Today, you see it all the time where too many newcomers demand we change our ways to accommodate their beliefs, and being who we are, we too often agree." He tore off a piece of sourdough flatbread, dipping it in something else delicious. "Let me ask you something, Father. If our society is so bad that it needs to be changed, then why does everyone want to come to America or to Europe? And why would you want to change things so that it's like your former home? If things were so good there, why did you leave?"

Amanuel nodded slowly. "I hear what you are saying, though I must admit I've never given it much thought. I never experienced your world until this week, and what I saw was both fascinating and terrifying. Your reliance on technology is something I don't understand, nor do I desire to, though"—he motioned toward the equipment they had brought—"I do feel a little hypocritical saying that, as it is that very technology that is going to save the Ark. I do wonder, though, if it's these newcomers, as you call them, demanding change, or do they provide you with a window into how others around the world live, and it makes you question whether your way is the only way."

Acton regarded the old man for a moment as he let his words sink in. It was an interesting proposition, though he didn't agree with it. He decided to try being diplomatic. "Wise words, Father, and they're words to consider, obviously." He sighed. "I just get so frustrated when I see our great country being attacked by its own people, claiming we're so terrible because of mistakes made decades or centuries in the past. Let's move on. Let's stop punishing people for things they said or did decades ago, and recognize that people, and countries, can change for the better over time."

Amanuel wiped his mouth. "Do you think perhaps how you treat these newcomers today is reminding you of your nation's past, and you don't like what you see?"

Acton smiled slightly. This priest was extremely wise, posing questions that were deceptively simple, yet challenging. This was a man he would enjoy spending more time with, if only that were possible. "Perhaps, Father, though one of the problems facing Western civilization is the relatively new concept of multiculturalism. While I believe in embracing the best of all cultures, the fundamental flaw in the official definition of multiculturalism is the fallacy that *all* cultures are *equally* good, therefore we should embrace and tolerate all other cultures and their customs and beliefs."

"That sounds reasonable."

"In principle, yes, however the fallacy is that all are equal, when they are not. I refuse to believe that a culture that subjugates women, for example, is equal to mine, that forces women to cover themselves, or practices female genital mutilation, or sexual slavery, or is against democracy or a free press. I refuse to believe that those cultures are equally good as mine, and should be respected and tolerated within mine. That's not to say that everything about cultures different than ours is bad, and I'm also not saying that everything about our own is perfect. What I am saying is that we need to realize it's okay to say to another culture that some of their beliefs are wrong, and won't be tolerated within our own."

"Interesting. You mention female genital mutilation. Here we have another name for it, obviously. It is quite a common practice here. Widely accepted. You think it is bad?"

Laura nodded. "Barbaric, Father. Sorry, but female genital mutilation is something I can never support, nor can I believe any civilized person could."

"So, I am uncivilized?"

Acton jumped at the opportunity to make his point. "See, and that is exactly the type of argument we see across America today. We built our country on a certain set of values, and it made us the greatest country that history has ever known. And now we're supposed to believe that every other country in the world is equal to us culturally, and we should be ashamed if we feel pride in what we've accomplished and in our way of life that has made us the envy of the world. And if we express that opinion, we're attacked."

"Do you feel I'm attacking you?"

Acton chuckled. "Of course not, Father, and I hope you don't feel I'm attacking you. What I'm saying is that everyone is entitled to their own culture, but should that culture, or aspects of it, not be compatible with the country *you* decide to *move* to, it is *you* that should adapt, not everyone around you."

"And you think that because of this, your society will collapse?"

Acton shook his head. "No, it is merely a symptom of a bigger problem."

Laura put down her cup. "Don't get him started on the Internet. You'll never hear the end of it."

Acton laughed. "True. The age of anonymity is one of the major factors destroying our civilization. When trolls, hiding behind fake names, can destroy people's lives and careers, quite often over something misinterpreted, decades old, or simply an outright lie, you have a problem. Whatever happened to innocent until proven guilty?"

"That sounds disturbing."

"It is, Father. Our country is more polarized than I think it has been in generations, perhaps ever, and it has to stop, otherwise we face a very uncertain future."

"One where your society collapses?"

"Perhaps. Unfortunately, the country seems to be divided into two camps that each think the other is stupid, uninformed, or evil. How can you possibly have reasonable discourse if you think your opponent is a moron, or so evil they don't have the right to express themselves?"

Amanuel frowned. "I am but a simple man, but I would think that if one has water to quench one's thirst, food to satisfy any hunger, and loved ones to surround oneself with, then that is enough. Would you not agree?"

Acton smiled. "Of course, however it takes a healthy economy to provide that water and food, and it requires communities that respect each other, even if they disagree. How can you live a happy life when you hate the other half of society?"

"I've seen similar problems here. Troubles between our Christian and Muslim brothers. Perhaps all societies are doomed to conflict."

"Perhaps, but those two groups have fundamentally different belief systems. In America, we have families that won't sit down to dinner with each other at the holidays because of politics. How ridiculous is that?"

"To allow something to come between family, to the point where you wouldn't break bread together, is something I cannot fathom. I hope your people can find a solution."

Acton sighed. "I hope so too, though I'm not sure if there is one. Not with things the way they are." He grunted, thinking of the Luddites he had encountered when they discovered Atlantis. "Perhaps the world would be a better place without so much technology."

Laura continued picking at the food. "Just get rid of the Internet. Problem solved."

Acton chuckled. "There'd be a Millennial uprising! Maybe if it wasn't so anonymous. If people knew who you were when you posted, it might tone it down a bit."

"Doubt it."

"You're probably right. The media would just fill the gap, and you know how ridiculous they've become over the past decade. Can you imagine if the newsmen of the past knew that one day their paper or television station would only report one side of the news, then claim anything that contradicted them was fake news? Nobody even considers the possibility anymore that they could be wrong. If someone disagrees, they're lying, they're evil, they should be tossed from office or tossed in jail."

Laura grunted. "Or killed."

Acton jabbed a finger at her. "Exactly. And that's when you have societal collapse."

Amanuel regarded him for a moment. "It sounds to me that perhaps you too are filled with the hate that you disdain so much."

Acton's eyes bulged and his jaw dropped at the priest's statement. "I…" He wanted to defend himself, though wasn't sure what to say. He quickly replayed his rant, trying to find where he might have crossed the line, but couldn't see it. These were things he had said before, things his friends agreed with, things he knew others disagreed with. Was he just as bad as those he disagreed with so vehemently?

He couldn't be. Could he?

Yet he had just dropped a ton of vitriol on an Ethiopian priest who couldn't possibly fathom the problems he was describing, yet had asked questions so astute, and so simple, that he had to wonder if a reassessment of his own thinking might be in order.

He sighed. "Father, perhaps you're right. I hate what's becoming of my country, and I guess, perhaps, I hate those who I think are responsible, though I don't hate any one side."

Laura winked. "You hate both."

He chuckled, wagging a finger at her. "Nooo. I hate people on both sides, but not any one side. I guess it's the extremists on both. Those few percent on the far left and the far right that are ruining everything for everybody. I consider myself part of the silent majority—"

"Not so silent today."

He laughed. "Okay, you got me there. I just wish we'd stop just ignoring things, and instead challenge the idiocy that comes across our social media feeds. And instead of just turning off the news, express our opinions in a civil manner about the bias we see. Teach our children how to find out the truth, rather than have someone else's version of the truth forced down their throats."

Amanuel regarded him. "Perhaps the truth lies in turning back to God."

"Perhaps, though most people in America still believe in God." Acton's stomach growled, loud enough for everyone to notice.

Laura motioned toward it. "Perhaps you should shut your mouth and stuff it instead."

He patted Laura on the leg. "You're right. I've said too much."

"Yes, you have, and poor Father Amanuel is simply too polite to say it."

Acton laughed, turning toward the priest. "I'm sorry, Father, if I've offended you, or wasted your time. Sometimes I just get so passionate about things, I find it hard not to express them."

"My job is to listen, my son, and I'm afraid with the task entrusted to me so many years ago, confession, and simply listening, are things I rarely get to partake in. I must say, I found what you had to say fascinating, and illuminating. I pay little mind to what happens beyond the walls of my church, instead devoting my time to prayer and ritual. It is refreshing if not disturbing, to hear the problems of regular people, especially from a country so different than mine. I will pray for you, and your country, tonight, and hopefully God will find a way to unite you once again, rather than divide you further."

Acton smiled. "That would be appreciated, Father. I think we need all the help we can get." He stared at the food, his stomach grumbling once again, then smiled at Laura, still taking her fill. "I better eat before there's none left."

She shrugged. "I make no apologies for focusing on the task at hand."

Acton eyed her. "Wait a minute. Didn't you start this conversation?"

She grinned. "Yup. And I egged you on, as well."

Operations Center 3, CIA Headquarters
Langley, Virginia

"Sir, we're starting to get hits on the suspicious arrivals Tesfay sent us."

Leroux turned to Tong, tearing his eyes away from the aftermath of what had just played out on the streets of Aksum, including the execution of one of the hostiles by an Ethiopian National Defense Force officer. "What can you tell me?"

"So far, they're all serious players in the underground antiquities business. It's a who's who of people that the professors probably hate." Tong paused, her eyebrows rising. "Huh, we've got some familiar faces here."

Leroux turned to the screen as she brought up the files. "Our Russian friends from Athens. That can't be good. Were they in that shootout we just witnessed?"

Tong shook her head. "No, it looks like they were an ISIS-linked group, and a South African group. I don't think we need to worry about either of them anymore."

Child agreed. "Ya think? They just wiped each other out. If only it were that easy every time."

Tong ignored him. "I think we're dealing with three remaining groups, including our Russians, unless more arrive. Unfortunately, they all have a propensity for violence, and are all likely well-armed."

Leroux nodded. "Okay, check for any more unscheduled flights into Aksum, just in case. I doubt any of them will be flying commercial."

"Yes, sir."

Leroux stared at the images of those that remained. "If they find out where the professors are, they won't hesitate to kill them, though the Russians have shown some restraint in the past."

Child grunted. "If that's not out of character, I don't know what is."

Leroux chuckled. "Agreed. Get the files on these guys to Delta so they know what they might be facing."

"Yes, sir," replied Tong.

"How do these guys know where they're going?"

Leroux turned to Child. "Excuse me?"

"Well, they can't know more than we do, right? You've got all these guys showing up here because they were able to see Professor Palmer's name and the delivery address for the generator on the invoice. Now they're all in position, hoping to get some sort of intel on where the professors are, right?"

"That's a reasonable assumption."

"And we know they got their intel off the Dark Web, all from the same source."

"Right. Where are you going with this?"

Child spun, staring at the ceiling. "Why don't we just send them all to the wrong place?"

Leroux stared at him for a moment then a smile slowly spread. "I like it. What did you have in mind?"

"Maybe we kill two birds with one stone."

Ganno Residence

South of Aksum, Ethiopia

Ganno embraced his two brothers, Theodros and Baruch, everyone awaiting him in his humble home all smiles and excited to see him despite only having been away for a few days.

It was the longest any of the brothers had been apart.

He sat, his wife bringing him water. He squeezed her hand. "It's good to see you."

"It's been too long. Don't go away like that again."

Ganno chuckled. "I would have thought a break from me would be appreciated."

She gave him a look as she placed food out for their guests. "I guess I enjoy the difficulties you bring."

Ganno roared with laughter, the others joining in before attacking the food. His wife discretely excused herself, knowing the conversation about to happen wasn't for her ears.

"So, bring me up to date."

Theodros swallowed. "The professors are here, with Father Amanuel. They were taken to its current location with their equipment, and have been there since. Two workers left about half an hour ago for some reason. We're not sure why."

Ganno pursed his lips as he leaned back. "So then, we can safely assume that not only has the secret of the Ark's existence been revealed, but they have also been shown it."

Theodros frowned, a long sigh escaping. "I can't see any other possible interpretation of what we've observed."

Ganno shook his head, his food forgotten. "Which means the Keepers have broken their vows."

Theodros nodded. "Yes, but from what we can tell, these professors are here to help preserve the Ark, not take it."

"Yes, that fact has been established. We actually found the invoices for their equipment purchases. However, the fact they know it exists means they must be eliminated."

Theodros regarded him. "Why? So far, they've told no one."

"Until today, they had nothing to tell beyond the fact a crazy priest from Ethiopia showed up on their doorstep. Today, they've actually seen it, they have something tangible they can speak of. And these are respected people. People will listen, at least enough to flood the area with treasure seekers. And if we keep killing anyone who gets close, it will quickly be known there actually *is* something to hide." He shook his head. "No, the moment the professors are finished their work, they must be eliminated so the truth can be contained. Agreed?"

Theodros nodded, along with the others, though more than he would have hoped appeared reluctant. And he understood, he supposed. This would be the first time any of them would kill to fulfill their duty. They were a safeguard against the failure of the Keepers, and the priests had always done their duty throughout history, with the one exception during the war. But today would be the first time they would shed blood in the history of their order.

But the Sons of Tamrin would fulfill their duty.

No matter how distasteful it was.

"Praise be to Menelik and Tamrin, and to our Lord, Jesus Christ."

Aksum, Ethiopia

"Hey, Alexie, look at this." Utkin waved his tablet without giving Tankov a chance to see what he was talking about. "We've got another posting from our moron about where the professors are. He wants half-a-million for the answer. He claims he's got exact coordinates, and he's giving it to anyone who pays. No bidding, no single winner."

Tankov grunted. "So, it's a race to the finish. What the hell, pay the man. Let's see what he has for us."

Utkin tapped away then handed the tablet to Tankov, a map displayed with their position relative to the purchased coordinates. "Well, it's in the area where our trusty Internet says the Ark is rumored to be."

A convoy of competitors whipped past them soon followed by another.

Utkin frowned. "We're going to have company."

Tankov nodded. "Yeah. Let's hold back and let them fight it out among themselves. We'll mop up what's left then take the Ark for ourselves."

"What about the professors?"

Tankov chewed his cheek for a moment, contemplating the future of the two educators who had cost them so much. He sighed. "I like them. Especially the woman. I want to marry her."

Utkin grinned. "Kill the husband and she's back on the market."

The men laughed, Tankov joining in. "True, but it'll have to be one of you. I can't have her hating me, it would just make our marriage difficult."

Utkin leaned in, staring at him. "You could change your face again."

Tankov ran his fingers over his face, staring at it in the rearview mirror, the only thing familiar his eyes. "I don't know. I'm just starting to get used to this one."

"It *is* one of your better ones, that's for sure. Then again, you always were a handsome devil."

Tankov gave him a look.

"I'm serious. It's the confidence. You could look like a pig's ass and you'd come off looking good."

Tankov turned to face him. "Arseny, are you trying to get into my pants?"

Utkin met his stare. "Is it working?"

Tankov roared with laughter as did the others, punching his friend on the shoulder. He put the vehicle in gear and pulled from the side of the road. "Okay, we've waited enough. Let's go kill what's left of the competition."

Approaching Ethiopian Airspace

Command Sergeant Major Burt "Big Dog" Dawson sat near the rear of the plane, staring at the fuselage opposite, as the others caught a few minutes shuteye. He was tired like they all were, their last op a success though trying.

Who knew Iranians didn't like strangers in their midst?

Normally none of that bothered him, and it didn't today. It was his new orders. He wasn't a very religious man, though he did consider himself Christian, and hopefully a good one at that. Beyond watching Raiders of the Lost Ark multiple times, he'd never given the Ark a second thought. Even then, it had never really occurred to him that it was real. It was more a movie prop than something out of the Bible.

And that's what had him so conflicted. Obviously, those up the chain, including the President, a man he had tremendous respect for, believed in the possibility enough to not only commit resources to its recovery or destruction, but to put lives on the line.

His and his men, as well as those who might get in their way.

What if they had to kill the priests? They wouldn't if the men didn't provide armed resistance, but what if they did? What if they had guns and fought back? Killing terrorists and truly bad guys was his business, and he never shed a tear or lost a wink of sleep when he killed one or a dozen of them.

But priests?

Even if armed, what was their crime? Protecting something sacred, something they believed in deeply, from thieves—him and his men— trying to steal that which wasn't theirs.

If they resisted with lethal force, he'd have to figure out some alternative to killing them.

"What's up, BD?"

He flinched, so lost in thought, he hadn't noticed his best friend and second-in-command, Master Sergeant Mike "Red" Belme, approach. He pointed at a nearby seat. "Take a load off."

Red sat and leaned forward, his elbows on his knees. "You look a bit off."

"It's nothing."

"Bullshit. I know you better than that."

Dawson grunted. "Okay, let's put it this way. It's nothing I can talk about."

Red frowned. "Opsec?"

"Exactly."

"Ahh, the burdens of command."

"You have no idea."

Red leaned back, stretching out his legs and folding his arms. "Is it the fact the professors have found the Ark of the Covenant?"

Dawson bolted upright. "How the hell do you know that?"

Red's eyes bulged. "Holy shit, I'm right?"

Dawson cursed, having fallen for the oldest trick in the book, delivered by his best friend and second-in-command. "You tricked me."

Red shook his head. "No, honestly, I was joking. Niner looked up archaeology conspiracy theories in Ethiopia, and Google came up with the Ark."

Dawson shook his head, his frown deep. "Remind me next time to shut down Internet access."

Red grinned. "They'll riot."

Dawson grunted. "Probably."

Red leaned closer, lowering his voice. "So, umm, are we on the Indy side of this? I mean, are we the good guys?"

Dawson sighed. "I hope so, but I have a bad feeling we're Belloq on this one. The only difference is we're stealing the Ark for America instead of Nazi Germany."

"This is insane. Do the brass actually think this thing works?"

Dawson shook his head. "My understanding is they think if there's even the remotest possibility, it can't be allowed to fall into the wrong hands."

"I see their point. If it does work, and the wrong side has it, like the Russians, it could be chaos. They could march across Europe, and there'd be nothing we could do to stop them." Red's eyes widened. "It could mean nuclear war."

Dawson nodded. "That's not what really worries me. I just can't see it being real. But what happens if a group of fanatics gets their hands on it, then decide to destroy it publicly? What would the reaction of Christians around the world be? Could it trigger a holy war?" He shook his head. "I think the safest thing is to just grab the damned thing, crate it up, and shove it in Hangar 18, never to be seen again."

Red's head slowly bobbed. "Agreed. Let's just hope that's what our President has planned for it. What's that old saying? Curiosity killed the cat?"

Dawson grunted. "There's something about Pandora's Box that has me more worried."

Aksum, Ethiopia

Tesfay pushed his newly acquired wheels as hard as he dared. His truck, now shot up, he knew. He knew its limitations, its capabilities, its quirks. This piece of junk pickup truck? He knew nothing beyond what it cost him to rent from a local for the day.

Too much.

But he had been desperate, with little time, and was lucky to have found anything.

He was heading for the last known position of Ganno, Control having sent him the coordinates only minutes ago. He was certain Ganno wasn't with the professors, as Control reported it was a house, not a church, that he had been seen entering. But Ganno's men would know where the professors were, and would likely lead him right to them.

He noticed his wounded arm getting tired and cursed as he let go of the wheel slightly, the vehicle heading to the right, the wheels far out of alignment.

This is going to be a shit drive.

He punched the steering wheel, wondering how he had been made. Control had confirmed the vehicle that had shot him up had left with Ganno, so it was his people that had made him. The only thing he could think of was that he had been spotted while he waited, then when he pulled out after Ganno, his men took action.

It could have been worse.

Normally they would have killed him, and the fact they hadn't, perhaps said something about the type of men they were dealing with. Perhaps these weren't insane murderers like he was used to dealing with, but instead, good men doing something they might find distasteful, though had no choice in.

Like himself. He had risked his life to save that little girl, now reunited with a thankful mother. Yet he wouldn't hesitate to kill a target if ordered to do so, as long as he was certain that target was bad.

He had to have faith in his handlers.

He hit a rut in the road and battled to regain control before skidding to a near halt, his speed less than half of what he'd like. He checked his watch and cursed. He had fifteen minutes to get into position. That might not be a problem in Texas, but here, where random roadblocks of military or armed gangs could appear with no warning, it was an entirely different thing.

Not to mention the road conditions.

He cleared a rise and cursed, jamming on his brakes. A roadblock, as feared, lay ahead. He grabbed the camera and adjusted its telephoto lens, peering at the barricade, and more importantly, who was manning it.

And cursed again, a group of men climbing into a vehicle, obviously with plans to confront him should he turn around.

He activated his comm. "Control, Whiskey-Alpha-Four here, come in, over."

"This is Control, go ahead, over."

"Umm, can you give me a hand here? I've confirmed they're not government. It's a local gang, over."

"Understood. Stand by."

Tesfay watched as the vehicle pulled away, loaded with half a dozen armed men. He put his truck in reverse, just in case.

Then smiled as two missiles streaked past him, hammering the illegal roadblock, two massive fireballs destroying everything and everyone in front of him.

Clearing his path.

"Thanks, Control, I owe you one."

"Any time, Whiskey-Alpha-Four."

Ganno Residence

South of Aksum, Ethiopia

"We've got company!"

Ganno, prepping to join the others, spun on his heel as Theodros rushed through the front door. "Who?"

"I don't know. Four vehicles. Two to the north, two to the south. All armed."

"Soldiers?"

Theodros shook his head. "No, the guys to the north look white, and the south look Middle Eastern. We must have been followed."

"How? You said you neutralized the tail, and we had an escort vehicle trail us by more than a kilometer."

Theodros threw up his hands. "I don't know! He had friends? Does it matter?"

Ganno grunted, shrugging his AK-47 over his shoulder. "No, it doesn't."

Theodros ushered him out the door and toward their awaiting vehicle. "We need to get you out of here."

Ganno grabbed his brother by the arm. "No, we must all go."

Theodros shook his head. "They'll just follow us if we do. You go, we'll engage them so you can escape. Rendezvous with the others and send help."

Ganno embraced his brother, bowing to Baruch as he rushed the women, including his wife, away to safety at another house a short distance away. If these new arrivals were after him, they should ignore the women, unless they were true barbarians.

Gunfire erupted from one of his men, the two hostile positions opening up with what sounded like far superior firepower. He hopped in the already running truck and slammed it in gear, flooring it then popping the clutch. The vehicle surged forward and down a rise, immediately providing him with some cover. He glanced to his right to see his wife and the others running toward the shelter of their neighbor's house, and sighed in relief as he spotted his children waving at them, safely out of range.

They would survive the day.

He just wondered if their uncles would.

Please, Lord, take care of my family and friends.

Tankov hammered on the brakes, bringing them to a halt. Utkin handed him binoculars and he surveyed the area, a smile spreading. It was exactly as he had hoped. There was a three-way gun battle unfolding, with all sides taking losses. All they would have to do is wait, then clean up the mess, with hopefully somebody in the house that seemed to be the primary target—and an exact match to the GPS coordinates they had just paid handsomely for—surviving the day to answer their questions.

Utkin pointed to their left. "Look."

Tankov turned to see a truck racing away, billowing dust behind it, there little doubt as to who its lone occupant was. "That's our guy."

"What makes you think that?"

"Because he's alone. If they were just trying to escape, that truck would be loaded with people. Instead, these guys stayed behind to give him a chance to get away."

Utkin nodded. "Sounds right. So, what are we going to do?"

"Play Follow the Leader. There's nothing to learn here beyond what we already have."

Utkin eyed Tankov. "And what's that?"

"That the GPS coordinates were bullshit."

Utkin's eyebrows shot up. "What makes you say that? There's obviously something going on here."

"Yes, but we're being used. There's no church here. There's just a house. The Ark isn't here, and there's no way the professors are here." Tankov shook his head. "We were led here, probably to have us take out whoever lives in that house."

Utkin frowned. "So that guy we've been paying was lying?"

Tankov shook his head. "No, I don't think that's what's going on here. He's too stupid to come up with something like this."

"Then what?"

"I think we're being played."

"You mean there's no Ark?"

Tankov shrugged. "I don't know, perhaps, perhaps not, but somebody else is involved, and with those two professors in the mix, I think I know who it is."

"Who? The American government?"

"Yup." Tankov stuck his head out the window, staring up at the sky.

"So, we're being watched?"

Tankov leaned back in. "Absolutely."

"Then what are we going to do?"

"Follow the leader, and see how things play out." He raised a finger. "But watch your backs. Special Ops could already be on the ground."

Dawson touched down and spun, hauling in his chute as the rest of the team landed around him. Their local contact, a man named Tesfay, jogged over to greet them, a ridiculously inadequate pickup truck the only transport in sight.

"Are you Mr. White?"

Dawson nodded. "Mr. Tesfay?"

"Yes, sir."

He pointed at the truck. "*This* is our transport?"

"Sorry, I had something bigger, but they made me and shot it up. This was the best I could do." He beckoned them to follow him. "Don't worry. It's not far. You won't be uncomfortable for long."

Niner smacked Dawson on the arm. "Forget comfort." He jerked a thumb at the massive Atlas. "If he gets in the back of this thing, we won't be going anywhere."

Atlas' impossibly deep voice cheerfully replied. "Don't worry, little man, if we need traction, we'll just put you under the tires."

Niner shoved the big man into the back of the truck as the others piled in, the shocks creaking in protest, the tires and frame getting disturbingly close. Dawson climbed into the passenger seat and slammed the door shut as Niner climbed over the hood and onto the roof. His head suddenly poked in the driver side window.

"No sudden stops, okay? I'd hate to damage the paint job."

Dawson reached over and shoved the man's face back outside. "Ignore him."

Tesfay started the truck and put it in gear, gently easing it forward, the engine struggling with the weight. It took longer than any would have liked, but they were soon in second gear, then third, and at least traveling faster than they would on foot.

Dawson's comm squawked.

"Zero-One, Control. Stand by for new coordinates."

Operations Center 3, CIA Headquarters

Langley, Virginia

"Did he just look out the window and up at us?"

Leroux laughed, Child absolutely correct. The Russian they had identified as Alexie Tankov had clearly done just that. "I think we've been made."

Laughter rippled through the room.

"Okay, warn Delta that the Russians didn't fall for the bait, and are aware they're being watched."

Tong relayed the message, then held up a finger. "Sir, interrogators in New York say they got a number from Fida, but it's not working. They think it's a satphone and might be turned off."

"Okay, try and track where it's been and keep monitoring for it, but I don't think we're going to need it. My guess is it belongs to Ganno, someone Ganno is planning on meeting, or someone in that house that's being hit. Those guys he left behind are obviously providing him with cover to escape, which means he's not only important, he's got somewhere important to be."

"Wherever the Ark is?" offered Child.

"Exactly. I'm betting he's going to lead us directly to the professors and whatever they're trying to preserve." He turned to Tong. "How far is Delta from Ganno's current position."

"Less than ten kilometers."

"Okay, tell them to get a wiggle on, or the Russians could get there first."

Child groaned. "Uh oh."

Leroux looked at him. "What?"

"I think we've got another problem bigger than the Russians." He pointed at the screen and Leroux turned.

And cursed.

"This just got a whole lot more complicated."

Ganno Residence

South of Aksum, Ethiopia

Captain Mussa held up a fist, bringing the column to a halt. They were several dozen now, all trusted, reliable men. And all but his sergeant completely in the dark as to why they were here. He stepped out of his truck and surveyed the area. Three positions were firing upon each other, two made up of foreigners, their target a house.

"They obviously think they know something." He pointed at the foreigners to the south. "Take out that position, surround the rest."

"Yes, sir!"

His second-in-command deployed the men, the fifties on their technicals opening up on the unsuspecting position made up of what appeared to be Middle Eastern men, their number down to four before his men opened fire.

And then there were none.

The second position turned their attention to the new arrivals, and several of his men went down, the others returning fire, eliminating all but two, who quickly dropped their weapons.

Mussa climbed back in. "Let's go."

His sergeant had them at the second position in moments, and Mussa stepped out, drawing his sidearm. He pointed it at the first survivor. "Where's the Ark?"

The man spat at him. "Go to hell."

Mussa put two rounds in his chest then adjusted his aim, addressing the lone survivor. "Where's the Ark?"

The man held his hands out in front of him, his eyes wide with fear. "I don't know! We were told it was here!"

"Then you're of no use." Two more rounds in the chest and Mussa motioned for his men to head for the house. He stopped near the front door and holstered his weapon. "Come out now, or die horribly painful deaths!"

It took a few moments, but eventually four men emerged, their hands up. Mussa stepped up to the first man. "Where is the Ark?"

"The what?"

Mussa drew his weapon and put a bullet in the man's head, stepping over to the next man, now trembling.

"I-I don't know!"

Another round to the head. He moved to the last two, both barely boys. "The first to answer lives. The other dies."

Both stared at each other then pointed, a set of fresh tracks visible leading away from the house. "Follow him!" "That way!"

Mussa sighed, shaking his head. "You both answered at the same time. That makes it difficult." He aimed at one, then the other, then the first. "I can't decide." He shot the first one, and the second smiled, if only for a moment.

Then he shot him too.

Mussa headed for his vehicle. "Let's go!"

Unknown Location

South of Aksum, Ethiopia

"Finally!"

Acton struggled to his feet, his muscles cramping as the two men returned carrying long poles, wrapped in gold, the fakes worth a fortune if they were built to the same specifications as described in the Bible. He stood back and let Laura take command.

"Okay, let's remove the original poles, *very* carefully."

Amanuel relayed the instructions and his men removed the first with ease, the second, broken one, with more trepidation, though successfully keeping it in one piece.

"Okay, now slide the new ones in." She watched, then gestured to the others. "Everyone in position."

Guns were put on the floor, and their guards became bearers, though it was clear there weren't enough. They had six men, but needed a minimum of eight. Acton stepped up, pairing with one of the odd men out, and Father Amanuel made for the final pairing when Laura held up a hand. "Allow me, Father. You guide us."

The elderly man smiled knowingly, and graciously took her up on her offer.

"On three," said Laura, Amanuel counting off in the local dialect, and holding up his fingers for his guests' benefit. They all lifted at once, and Acton nearly died from shock, the Ark unfathomably heavy. And he wasn't sure why he was surprised. It was constructed from solid wood and gold, and would easily weigh more than a thousand pounds.

And that explained why the poles were so long.

There should be a dozen carrying this.

But they didn't have far to go, and with a lot of grunting, groaning, cursing, and moaning, they managed to move it the several feet needed, and onto the newly constructed platform.

Acton collapsed on the floor along with the others, gasping for breath. After several minutes of recovery, Laura resumed guiding the process, having Amanuel's men exchange the fake poles with the genuine articles, leaving the broken one as it was, their object today not to repair, but to preserve.

They raised the plexiglass walls into place, sealing the sides, then installed the top, locking it in place. Electrical and data cables were hooked up, and Laura smiled at the room. "Well, here goes nothing." She activated the system from a control panel mounted to the side of the self-contained unit, and sighed. "It works!"

Acton winked at her. "You sound surprised."

"Well, one never knows." She beckoned Amanuel over. "Okay, the system is running and everything is looking good. It will take a little while for the humidity and temperature levels to reach optimum, but if you keep this running, the Ark should last another three thousand years."

Amanuel smiled. "Let's hope it won't be that long before man is united under one God, and the Ark is long forgotten."

"Let's hope." She patted her handiwork. "The equipment will need to be maintained, and changed out every ten years, especially in these conditions. As you've seen, it was pretty easy to set up. You should be able to just order replacement parts yourselves, and swap out the units. Brief exposure won't damage the Ark, but never lift it by the original poles. I'll leave you all the part numbers you'll need, along with descriptions so in the future, the modern equivalent can be bought."

Amanuel smiled, walking around the chamber, running his hand along its surface. "I'm glad you're thinking long term. I wouldn't have thought of that."

Laura chuckled. "We're archaeologists. Everything is long term for us."

Half a dozen men rushed into the room, one whispering something to Amanuel, a deep frown creasing the man's face as Acton wondered why the additional muscle couldn't have arrived ten minutes ago.

"Problem?"

Amanuel tilted his head. "For me, no, but for you, I'm afraid so."

Ganno dropped to his stomach and peered over the rise at the church carved into the bedrock below. He had grown up with these creations, and despite seeing them his entire life, he never ceased to be impressed.

For he had never stepped inside one.

The leaders of the Sons of Tamrin never did, though members of their order did when the need arose.

"Status?"

"Our man on the inside says they've just finished their work. The generator is powered up and the Ark is inside its new crate, or whatever you want to call it."

Ganno smiled, sighing. "Then it will be safe from now on. This is a good thing. We owe the professors our gratitude."

"You should thank them before you shoot them."

He frowned at the wry smile of his underling. "I take no pleasure in killing them. It is my duty. *Our* duty. The secret must be preserved, or the prophecy can never be fulfilled."

"Maybe it's not meant to be."

He eyed the man he considered a friend. "Jesus Himself said it."

"Yes, but—"

"But nothing. We have a job to do. Are you up to it?"

"Of course."

"Then what must happen?"

"The professors must die."

"Exactly."

"Hey, sir, look!"

Ganno looked where one of his men was pointing.

What the hell is this?

"*They* are here, aren't they?"

Amanuel nodded at Acton. "Yes."

"Do you have any weapons?"

"Only those my men carry, but they've never fired them."

Acton's eyes widened. "Never?"

"There's never been a need."

Laura stepped forward. "Well, we have. Give us the weapons and ammo, then get out of here."

Amanuel shook his head. "I can't leave the Ark."

"You'll have to." She put a hand on the man's shoulder. "It's that order you warned us of, isn't it?"

"Yes."

"Then they're not here to destroy the Ark, they're here for us. Go now, while you can."

Amanuel shook his head. "I will try to reason with them first. Stay here."

He rushed from the room and Laura took after him, Acton following.

But it was too late. The old man was already halfway up the stairs to the surface, and they couldn't risk exposing themselves unarmed.

"He'll be okay," said Acton. "Like you said, they're not here for him."

They returned to the chamber containing the Ark to find a pile of weapons and ammo in the middle of the room, the guards nowhere in sight.

Acton cursed. "Thanks for nothing!"

Laura patted him on the shoulder then dropped to her knees, taking a quick inventory. He joined her, picking out the best looking AK-47 he could and handing it to her as she sorted out the magazines, searching for those that were fully loaded.

There weren't enough.

She sighed. "So, what are we going to do?"

Acton shrugged. "Die, I guess." He stared at the Ark, a thought occurring to him. "Umm, do you think *He* might help us?"

Laura stuffed mags in every pocket she had. "I'm still not convinced *He* has anything to do with that thing. Besides, I wouldn't have a clue on how to use it."

Acton shrugged. "In Raiders they lifted the top off and all hell broke loose."

She gave him a look. "Something tells me it isn't as simple as that."

Acton sighed. "Leave it to God to make things difficult."

Laura grinned. "Now He won't help us for sure." She wagged a finger. "You really need to watch that mouth of yours."

Acton flushed. "Did I go too far?"

"At home with me or our friends, no problem. With a priest from Ethiopia, who knows nothing but hardship, your argument came off as a little First World."

Acton grunted, loading his own pockets with ammo. "I guess so. If we survive this, remind me to apologize again."

Laura rose, slinging a spare AK-47 over her shoulder, another gripped in her hands. "I think he's forgiven you."

Acton stuffed the only handgun in his waist. "What makes you say that?"

"Because he's going out there to face *our* enemy, not his."

Acton felt sick to his stomach. "Sometimes I'm a putz."

Laura patted his cheek. "But I still love you."

He grinned. "One last shag before it's all over?"

"You're incorrigible. This is a church."

Acton's eyes widened, having forgotten the location of their predicament. "I'm definitely going to hell."

Father Amanuel walked across the hard stone surrounding the church, toward the armed men lining the ridge to its north. Then stopped. One of them rose, a man he recognized from the area, a man named Ganno.

"You're a member of the Sons of Tamrin?"

Ganno walked toward him, his weapon in hand, and nodded as he came to a stop in front of him. "I am."

"I must admit I'm relieved. From what I know of you, you are an honorable man, supporting a good wife and fine children."

"Thank you, Father, your words do me honor."

"Then please do me the honor of leaving this place."

"You know I can't do that. Not until my business here is done."

"And that business is?"

"To preserve the secret."

"By killing the professors."

Ganno nodded, the pain in his eyes evident. "I'm afraid so."

"These are good people, my friend. In fact, they've helped us preserve that which is so important to both of us. They've done nothing wrong."

"No, they haven't. You did. And now they must pay for your mistake."

Amanuel's heart hammered and his stomach flipped, for Ganno was right. It *was* his mistake. Yet it had been necessary. "I had no choice. The Ark needed to be preserved."

"You could have gained the knowledge by other means."

Amanuel shook his head. "No, it was falling apart. God only knows how much longer it would have lasted."

Ganno held up a hand. "Father, are the professors inside?"

There was no point in lying. "Yes."

"Are any of your people?"

"Yes."

"Then I suggest you leave, otherwise you may get hurt."

Amanuel thought of what Laura had said. "They won't just let themselves be killed. You might die."

"I'm willing to die in service to my Lord Jesus Christ, as a Son of Tamrin." He smiled slightly. "And I don't think two professors from America are going to be much trouble."

Amanuel stepped closer. "Perhaps. Unless they have God on their side."

Ganno's eyes flared and he took a step back, clearly shaken, though he quickly regained his composure, or at least a semblance of it. "You've got two minutes, Father, then we're coming in."

"We've got a final location," said Leroux as Dawson covered his ear, the roar of the protesting engine loud. "We think it's going down at the coordinates we just sent you."

Dawson checked his phone, confirming receipt. He pulled up the map showing their location relative to the new coordinates. "Okay, we're about ten minutes from there at the pace we're going. How many are we facing?"

"Looks like about two dozen surrounding the location on all sides."

"We should be able to handle it."

"One other thing. Well, actually two. Those Russians are about five minutes out, and you've got about fifty Ethiopian regulars headed your way, about fifteen minutes out."

Dawson cursed. "Hardware?"

"Mostly AKs, but they've got four fifties mounted on technicals."

"No heavy armor?"

"No."

"Any chance of getting help?"

"Already on the way, but they're thirty minutes out. You're going to be on your own for at least fifteen minutes."

Dawson cursed. "Well, tell those flyboys to put the pedal to the metal or they're going to miss all the action."

"Roger that, Zero-One, Control, out."

Dawson pointed to the road ahead, if you could call it that. "Let's speed this beast up otherwise we're going to be in it up to our eyeballs."

Tesfay nodded, pressing a little harder on the accelerator. "I'll try, but she might blow."

Suddenly they hit a rut, jerking them to the side, and Niner cried out, skidding down the windshield and over the side. He rolled out of the way and Dawson watched with a grin as the man jumped to his feet and gave chase.

"Should I stop?"

Dawson shook his head. "No time. He'll catch up."

And he did, reaching the opened gate of the pickup truck, his hand outstretched.

Atlas swatted it away.

"Come on, asshole, pull me in!"

Atlas smacked the outstretched hand again.

"I'm going to shoot you the next chance I get!"

Atlas grabbed the hand and hauled Niner in with one impressive pull, swinging him onto the heap of bodies crammed into the bed of the truck. Niner struggled to find a place to put a foot that wasn't in someone's groin, then stabbed a finger toward Atlas.

"I'm making out with your sister the next time she's in town."

Atlas grabbed the finger, twisting. "You should know it's my *mama* that thinks you're cute!"

Acton watched as Amanuel descended the steps, resignation of their impending doom written on his face. "I'm sorry, my children, but I failed. You are, I'm afraid, on your own."

Acton shook the man's hand. "Get out of here, Father, before it's too late."

Laura took the man's hand. "It's okay, Father, we don't blame you."

272

The old man smiled, then made the sign of the cross, blessing them both. "Just in case."

Acton chuckled. "Go, before it's too late."

Amanuel nodded then disappeared inside. Acton rushed to the top of the stairs, keeping low as he neared the surface, flush with the ground.

Laura knelt behind him, her assault rifle gripped comfortably. "So, what do we do? Surrender?"

He vehemently shook his head. "There's no way I'm letting them take you alive. God only knows what they'd do to you."

"Well, I'm not letting them take you alive either. You're a handsome man, and maybe some of them are into that kind of thing."

Acton laughed. "Never thought of that." He erased his smile as he stared at her. "Save one bullet for yourself, in case it comes to that." His chest ached at the thought, and he leaned in, kissing her hard, thinking of everything they had been through over the years, then wiped away the threatening tears as he took aim at the ridgeline, wishing he had a Glock and an MP5 instead of an aging AK-47 that had seen better days.

Let's just hope these things can still fire.

Ganno waved his hand then pointed, his men rising and slowly advancing from all sides on the church carved into the ground ahead. There had been no sign of Amanuel or his men leaving, and he wasn't happy about that. If they fought back, then so be it, though he prayed they were simply hiding inside, consumed by prayer.

I hope you know what you're doing, Father.

Gunfire erupted from the church, well-aimed, several of his men dropping from two directions. He hit the ground, returning fire, all positions opening up as half a dozen of his men writhed on the ground, bleeding out, or lay still, their souls already departed.

Whose side are you on, Lord?

Tankov cocked an ear, gunfire erupting in the distance. He smiled. "Sounds like the fun has already begun." He pointed to a dune ahead, Utkin now driving. "Head over there. It should provide good cover."

Utkin guided them behind the dune and the men exited the large SUV, crawling to the top. Tankov surveyed the area and Utkin pointed. "There are the professors."

Tankov didn't see them. "Where?"

"In that, I don't know, thing. See the square, carved into the ground?"

Tankov removed the binoculars and just looked with his bare eyes. "What the hell is that?"

Utkin shrugged. "I don't know. I can see some sort of stairs, though, leading down. That's where they've taken up position."

Tankov peered through the binoculars again, spotting them easily this time. "Got them. Looks like he's covering one and two, she's covering three and four. Looks like about two dozen hostiles, though a few seem to be out of commission."

"What should we do?"

Tankov sighed. "I really don't like seeing the numbers so uneven like that. It's hardly a fair fight. And I'd hate to see my future wife taken out like this."

"Your love life aside, if they somehow come out on top, they won't let the Ark go without a fight, and it will be us killing the professors."

Tankov frowned. "Okay, let's see what happens. Maybe the decision will be made for us. We're here for the Ark, not the professors. But let's get ready to take out whoever wins."

"Do you think they have a chance?"

"No. They'll be out of ammo any minute now. They're on single-shot for a reason."

"I think this is it," said Acton, taking Laura by the shoulders. "I love you!"

Tears burned her eyes as she stared at her husband for what would be the last time. Memories of their years together flooded her mind, and for a moment anger surged through her as she asked why God would let them die when there was so much evil in the world. "I love you too!"

He smiled at her. "See you on the other side?"

She nodded then gasped as tears flooded her eyes. He grabbed her and she held on to him as tightly as she could, breathing in his scent one last time before he let her go, jumping up and firing like the maddest, bravest man she had ever met. She joined him, flicking her weapon to full auto, emptying what few bullets she had left into the encroaching enemy.

Then heavy, distinctive gunfire erupted from her left.

What the hell?

Tankov rained bullets on the enemy, deciding he wasn't about to let two people he respected, regardless of them being rivals, die in this way. The enemy quickly figured out their position and returned fire, which was when his second position opened up on them. Caught in a crossfire, they were quickly mowed down, the last few racing for a technical and beating a hasty retreat.

The guns fell silent, and after a few moments, the professors rose, searching for their saviors.

He stood and waved, a smile on his face, a face neither of them had seen before.

"Who the hell is that?"

Laura shrugged. "I don't know. They don't look like Bravo Team."

Acton shook his head. "No, they don't. For all we know, they're here to steal the Ark."

"They did save our asses."

"Did they? Or did they just save their payday." Acton paused, staring at the man as he approached, recognizing the weapon. "I think they're Russian."

"You mean as in the ones who kidnapped us when they stole the Amber Room?"

"As in exactly them."

"If it is, we're in trouble. Ammo?"

"I'm empty."

"Me too."

Acton glanced at his wife. "I thought I told you to save one bullet?"

"You didn't."

He grinned. "I figured they'd oblige." He reached out from the stairwell they stood in and grabbed the nearest body, dragging it closer. A quick pat down revealed four magazines. He handed two back to Laura then reloaded.

"Are we taking them on?"

"We might not have a choice."

Laura took him by the arm. "But we do. We can walk away. Let them have it."

He stared at her. "Do you want the power of *God* in the hands of the Russians?"

"Of course not, but we don't know if this thing is real."

"You felt it just like I did!"

She shook her head. "I don't know what I felt."

"Then maybe you should get back in there and try again."

She gave him the stink eye. "Don't get snarky."

He sighed, closing his eyes for a moment. "You're right, I'm sorry. But I think it could be real. Yes, maybe it was all in my head, but if it wasn't, then we have to protect it from people like these guys."

Laura grunted. "Maybe we shouldn't have killed so many of the Sons of Tamrin."

Acton shrugged. "Well, I always wanted to go out in a blaze of glory." He nodded toward the approaching man. "Once again these Russians have ruined my plans."

"Professor Acton! Professor Palmer! So good to see you again."

Acton turned to face him, a frown on his face as he recognized the voice from Poland and Athens, confirming the man's identity.

"Now what?" asked Laura, her voice barely a whisper.

"Lie our asses off?"

"Do you think that will work?"

"Not a chance."

"Then what?"

"Pray for a miracle."

Ganno scrambled behind a cluster of boulders, his chest heaving as he gasped for breath. The few survivors from the surprise attack dropped around him, all in shock, all exhausted.

"What just happened? Who were they?" asked the youngest.

Ganno shook his head. "I don't know, but they're well-armed and know what they're doing."

"What do we do now? Call for reinforcements?"

Ganno looked at him. "Who? Almost everyone was here, and the fact no one has arrived from my house tells me they're all dead."

"Then what do we do?"

Ganno sighed, closing his eyes as his duty was clear, and after three thousand years, he would be the one forced to do it. "We have no choice. If these men are here, then they know about the Ark. Word is already out. We must fulfill our sworn duty."

Wide eyes and slack jaws surrounded him.

"Destroy the Ark?"

"I see no other choice."

"But how? We've lost the fight."

Ganno smiled at the young man. "We may have, but we haven't lost the war. Years ago, when we knew there might be need, our operatives infiltrated the four churches the Keepers use to hide the Ark in, and planted explosives, just in case they might ever be needed."

"You did? I mean, *we* did? Why don't I know about this?"

"Because you're a junior member, son. Eventually, you would have been told when the day approached that it might be your responsibility to fulfill our oath."

The boy nodded. "I understand, I guess." He looked around. "But how do we set off the explosives?"

"We ran wires to a safe distance." Ganno pointed to the south. "About one hundred meters that way. We just need to connect the detonator." He cursed as he remembered something. "And it's in my truck." He rose, peering out from between the rocks, his vehicle only a couple hundred yards away, though very close to where the new arrivals were. There were additional detonators at his house, and those of his brothers, but that was too far, especially on foot. He had no choice.

"Okay, I'm going to get the detonator. You stay here. If I don't make it back, one of you has to try again. We need that detonator, otherwise we fail in our duty." He rose. "Praise be to Menelik and Tamrin, and to our Lord, Jesus Christ."

Acton aimed his weapon at the ground, but in the general direction of their approaching savior. "That's close enough."

The Russian smiled, coming to a stop. "You don't trust me, Professor? We just saved your lives."

Acton gave him a look. "For entirely altruistic reasons, I'm sure."

"Why, is there something of importance here?"

Acton shook his head. "Not at all, just an old church we're visiting."

"And these men that tried to kill you?"

He shrugged. "No idea. They just showed up here, demanded we be handed over, and we decided not to go down without a fight."

"You were doing good. I was impressed."

Acton gave a slight bow. "Thank you."

"And that final act, jumping up and shooting madly into the crowd? That seemed either desperate or noble."

"Perhaps a little of both."

"I think you were sacrificing yourselves for something."

Acton shook his head. "Nothing so noble. We just didn't want to be captured by the likes of these."

The Russian nodded. "True. This part of the world isn't known for its civilized behavior toward prisoners." He stared at Laura, his eyes roaming her from top to bottom and back. "Especially when it comes to beautiful women." He returned his attention to Acton. "So, what are we going to do here? There are six of us, heavily armed, and two of you. We all know what lies inside that church."

Acton played dumb. "What?"

"The Ark of the Covenant."

"What makes you think that?"

The Russian chuckled. "Professor, I believe you've been out of communication for some time. At least five distinct groups of, shall we say, relic hunters, arrived here today, because someone spilled the beans for good old cash. Two wiped each other out at the airport, with the help of the Ethiopian military, two more were doing a good job of killing each other not far from here, and the fact they're not here yet tells me they succeeded, and now we're who's left in the game. We *will* take the Ark. You can either step aside and let us, or we can walk over your dead bodies and take it anyway." He raised his weapon. "What's it going to be?"

Acton retreated two steps down, slightly raising his weapon in response. "We just survived two against two dozen. I'm willing to take my chances on half a dozen."

The Russian sighed. "Very well. I really didn't want it to end this way." He abruptly raised his weapon, opening fire as Acton dove backward, taking Laura with him as they tumbled down the stone steps.

Tankov advanced, debating whether to toss a grenade down the stairs he was now seeing, but deciding against it as it might damage the Ark. A hail of gunfire erupted from the recessed stairs and he backed off.

"Professor, you're making this harder than it needs to be. Just drop your weapons and come out. You can still survive the day. I don't care about you. I only care about the Ark."

"How touching!"

Tankov chuckled.

"Why don't you come and get it?"

Tankov shook his head. "Very well, professor, you had your chance." He motioned his team forward, and they surrounded the stairwell on the three exposed sides. "One grenade, and you're both dead."

"One grenade, and you destroy the Ark. Something tells me your buyer won't be happy with that. "

Tankov sighed. "You're right." He removed a flashbang from his belt and popped the pin. "Sorry, professors, you're simply out of your league."

"Now."

Niner squeezed the trigger, putting several rounds at the feet of the Russians as the rest of Bravo Team rose from their hidden positions, surging forward and surrounding the hostiles.

Dawson aimed his weapon directly at the Russian Langley had identified as Alexie Tankov. "How about you put that pin back in there?"

Tankov cursed, slowly turning around, his hands rising as he stepped backward several paces. "And who the hell are you?"

"United States Army. I believe you're threatening the lives of an American citizen, and an ally." Dawson took another step closer. "As well as two good friends of mine."

"BD, is that you?"

Dawson stepped closer to the hole cut into the ground, his eyebrows popping slightly as he got an angle on it, a set of stairs revealed. "Secure yourselves, Doc, this should only take a moment."

"Roger that!"

Dawson flicked his MP5. "Drop your weapons, and we'll let you leave. Hesitate, you die."

Tankov regarded him. "You'd kill Russian citizens, just like that?"

Dawson shrugged. "Why not? Nobody will ever find your bodies."

Tankov eyed him. "You're here for the Ark, aren't you? Your President sent you here to retrieve it."

"I have no idea what you're talking about." He took another step closer, raising his weapon slightly. "Now, drop your weapons, and walk away. Last time I'm going to ask."

"Very well." Tankov dropped the flashbang and dove down the stairs, Dawson cursing as he turned away from the blast.

Ganno scrambled the last few feet as a loud blast erupted ahead. He pressed against the truck and peered through the windows, no evidence of an explosion visible.

Was it inside the church?

If it was, then his job might already be done, but he couldn't take that chance. He had to finish the job. He crawled inside and found the detonator in the glove compartment, where one was always kept just in case. He slithered back out, then headed for the wires hidden well away from the targeted churches, so they could be detonated without interference from the Keepers.

The Ark was moved regularly, switched with fakes that were spread throughout the area. Some were obvious, some were remarkably accurate.

Four to be exact.

And those were rotated so few ever knew which one was real, even among the Keepers and the Sons of Tamrin.

But the number of locations was limited, as it would involve too many people if more churches were used, which made the order's job easier.

He reached the cover of some nearby rocks and took a moment, his chest aching and stomach churning with the knowledge of what he was only moments away from doing. After all these years, it would be him who would destroy the precious relic, a gift from God Himself to His chosen people.

Yet along with the guilt that racked him was joy. The thought that because of him, because of what he was about to do, the prophecy would finally have a chance to come true, without the risk of the Ark becoming known to man ever again, sent shivers through his body.

"And just where do you think you're going?"

Ganno froze, the deep voice, impossibly deep voice, was followed by a foot shoved into his back, sending him sprawling on the ground. The detonator was still gripped in his hand, a hand now hidden under him. He slipped the device into his pocket.

"Get up."

The foot was removed and Ganno struggled to his feet, raising his hands over his head, his eyes widening at the massive man in front of him, equipped with state of the art gear that likely meant he was American.

"Let's drop the gun. Nice and easy now."

Ganno unslung the AK-47 from his back, slowly lowering it to the ground. The man kicked it aside. "Who are you?"

"I'm asking the questions."

Gunfire erupted to their left and the big man turned toward it. Ganno made a break for it but found his path blocked by an Asian man, half the size of the behemoth. A boot swiftly kicked Ganno in the balls and he dropped to the ground in agony.

"Didn't your mama teach you not to run away from strangers?"

The big man eyed the little one. "I think your mama and my mama need to have a talk."

More gunfire had this odd couple serious once more, the big man pointing at the truck.

"Let's handcuff him to that. We'll collect him later."

Ganno was hauled to his feet and led back to his truck, where the big man pulled out a plastic zip tie to secure him. The Asian shook his head.

"No, use handcuffs. He might have a knife in there somewhere."

"Good thinking."

"I'm not just a pretty face."

"When we get home, I'm going to mess that face up in the ring."

"What did I do to deserve that?"

"You asked my girlfriend if she was wearing panties."

"Only so you could get in them."

"Now I'm really going to mess you up."

The big man handcuffed him to the steering wheel, then they both bolted toward the action, leaving Ganno to watch helplessly as two of the oddest men he had ever encountered raced toward the secret he was sworn to protect.

"Well, that was stupid."

Dawson chuckled as he peered down the stairs to see the Russian staring up at the barrels of two assault rifles aimed at him, the professors alive and well, though Laura appeared to be in some pain. The Russian raised his hands and Acton quickly stripped him of weapons when gunfire erupted to Dawson's left.

He dove, rolling, then placed two rounds in the chest of his nearest target, Red doing the same on his right. It took only moments, and all five remaining Russians, including the one who had panicked and started the ill-advised firefight, were down, either dead or incapacitated.

He leaped to his feet and rushed forward, disarming his man, confirming what he had already suspected. The Russians were wearing body armor. "Disarm them, secure them, *then* treat them. They're wearing body armor."

His men executed his orders as Atlas and Niner appeared over the rise to his right.

"Everything good?" asked Niner as he came to a halt.

Dawson nodded. "What took you two so long?"

"We encountered that Ganno guy Langley told us about."

Dawson reached out and grabbed Atlas by the shoulder, turning him around slightly.

"Looking for something?" asked the big man.

"Just checking to see if you had strapped him on your back."

"Haw haw." Atlas jerked a thumb over his shoulder. "We handcuffed him to a truck."

"Okay, things are secure here, so go get—"

"Holy shit, BD!"

Dawson turned to where Spock was pointing and cursed. Dozens of Ethiopian regulars had just crested the rise, their fifties aimed at his team."

"This can't be good," rumbled Atlas.

Niner punched him on the shoulder. "Ya think?"

Red sauntered over in as non-threatening a manner as anyone could manage under the circumstances. "Do you think they're here for us?"

Dawson shook his head. "Nobody knows we're here."

"Then they're here for the, umm, thing?"

"Probably."

"So, we're in their way."

"I'd say that's an accurate assessment."

Red's head bobbed. "Do you think they'll let us go?"

"Unlikely."

"So, we're screwed."

"Could be."

"So, any idea on how to get unscrewed?"

Dawson nodded. "The church is the only cover, and they don't really have an angle on it from where they are." He glanced at his men, all on their feet, backing slowly away from the Russians now zip-tied and on the ground. "Everyone keep your weapons down, and slowly approach the edge while I distract them."

He activated his comm then grabbed one of the Russians, hauling him to his feet, only his pride and ribs wounded. He turned him to face the Ethiopians. "Is this who you want? We took them out for you. Let us leave, and you can take whatever you want." He lowered his voice as his men slowly edged toward the only cover in the area. "Control, ETA on that backup?"

"Five minutes, Zero-One."

"That's not going to be good enough. Drones?"

"Two, both armed. Choose your targets."

"Roger that. Anything with a fifty in the back. And tell those guys to try and not hit the same one twice."

Leroux chuckled. "I'll pass it on." There was a pause as one of the Ethiopians, apparently in charge, stepped out of his vehicle, his hands on his hips as he surveyed the area. "Engaging now."

Dawson turned his head slightly toward the Russian. "When they hit, get down those stairs if you want to live. Go for a weapon, I'll kill you myself."

The man glared at him, but nodded.

"You are a hostile force on Ethiopian territory, American. Surrender yourselves, and we may let you live."

May. How nice of him.

"Control, where are those—"

"Impact in five, four, three, two—"

Dawson shoved the Russian to the ground then jumped on top of him as two AGM-114 Hellfires slammed into the cluster of Ethiopian regulars. Screams and secondary explosions filled the air and Dawson leaped to his feet, leaving the Russian behind, as he raced for the cover of the church stairs, carved into the solid rock, his men already hopping over the edge and out of sight. The Russians still alive and mobile scrambled to join them as disorganized gunfire erupted from the Ethiopian position. He dove for the stairs, coming up slightly short, then rolled into the abyss, hands catching him before he hit the hard rock.

"Everybody good?" he asked as he was helped to his feet, a round of affirmatives greeting him. "Professors?"

"Peachy!" replied Acton from below.

"Good. Then let's hold this position until the cavalry arrives. Take out those fifties before they regroup."

Ganno flinched at the two massive explosions just out of sight of where the bastard Americans had left him. He tugged at his hand, trying to force his wrist through the handcuffs, but it was no use. He was running out of time. There was only one reason the Americans were here, and it was the same as the military personnel he had seen drive by his position minutes ago.

They both wanted the Ark.

The secret was out, and it had to be destroyed.

And there was no one left to do it but himself.

He still had the detonator. The wires to attach it to were only a couple of hundred feet from here, and with everyone distracted by the gun battle, he could fulfill his oath easily.

If only he could get loose.

He searched the vehicle for anything that might help, then stopped, a solution to his problem spotted lying on the back seat.

A horrible solution.

Please, Lord, give me strength.

Captain Mussa dropped to his stomach and drew his weapon, opening fire as the last few who remained in the open were shredded, though they appeared unarmed. He had a feeling they were dealing with two groups here, one victorious over the other.

He surveyed the area as the gunfire eased, then shook his head. Dozens of bodies were strewn about, including many locals.

Three groups?

It appeared half the country knew the Ark was here, as well as half the world.

That meant they had little time.

He rose, raising his arm and ordering his men forward. "No grenades! We can't risk what's inside!"

There were several puzzled glances, his men still in the dark, but they executed his orders, slowly advancing on the church that lay below. He turned to the remaining two technicals with fifties mounted in the back. "Separate those guns. We don't know what they hit us with, but they could be back."

He advanced with his men then raised his weapon as a head popped out from the sunken steps. He fired, his men joining in, but the man ducked in time.

A popping sound was heard from the enemy position and Mussa cursed. "Take cover!"

An explosive round slammed into the ground to his left, two of his men cut in half as he hit the dirt. Another pop and his men panicked as they raced for cover, none to be found.

This better be worth it!

Acton bound the Russian leader's hands behind his back with zip ties provided by Red, then shoved him inside the church and out of the way as Laura covered him. The surviving Russians were passed down, the process repeated, then they both covered them, freeing up the Delta personnel to engage yet another enemy hellbent on possessing the Ark.

Explosions overhead shook the entire area, and he warily eyed the structure they were now sheltering in as dust slowly settled around them. Dawson appeared in the doorway, startling him.

"You two got this?"

Acton nodded. "Yes."

"Good. Is there another way out of here?"

"Not that I know of."

"The Ark is here, isn't it?"

Acton's eyebrows popped. "You know about that?"

"Doc, everybody knows. You wouldn't believe the shitstorm that's been happening since you left."

Laura stepped forward. "I thought it was supposed to be a secret."

Dawson shrugged. "I don't know what to tell you, but somebody blabbed, and now every relic hunter on the planet is after it and converging on this area."

Acton glanced at the Russians. "They can't be allowed to find it."

"So, it *is* here."

"Yes."

Dawson's eyes bulged. "Umm, is it, ahh, real?"

Acton sighed, exchanging a glance with Laura. "Well, there's some debate surrounding that, but it's a definite possibility." He jabbed a finger at the action that continued overhead. "We can't let these people have it."

"My orders are to take the Ark into custody and bring it back to the United States."

Laura's eyes widened. "Are you kidding me? Why?"

"Because, Professor, if it's real and falls into the wrong hands, it could cause a war. And if it's not, and the wrong people have it, it could trigger a war regardless, just to get it back."

Acton shook his head. "What are you going to do with it?"

"*I'm* not going to do anything. The President wants it in American hands, then put away so no one can touch it."

Acton chewed his cheek, shaking his head. "Do you trust him?"

"I trust *him*, but who the hell knows who the next guy is going to be?"

A massive explosion shook the room and Acton ducked. "It might not matter if we don't survive this."

Dawson checked his watch then grinned. "Doc, I think it's about to rain."

Captain Mussa cowered behind one of his remaining vehicles as his men poured lead onto the enemy's position. They had plenty of ammo, and he had no doubt they would outlast what he presumed were Americans. The fact no more missiles had hit them meant any threat from the sky was over, whatever had fired the two missiles, probably drones, out of ammo.

They would be victorious in the end, and all he had to do was survive the battle and claim his reward.

But how would he sell it?

He'd have to talk to his brother. He'd know.

He'll want a cut.

Even if the bastard took half, it wouldn't matter. He would still be rich, and why not share it with family?

You could just melt it down for the gold.

That was an idea. It would simplify things, and if there was as much gold there as the legends suggested, he would still be a wealthy man, and could simply use it as he needed it, without it being traceable. Selling the Ark itself could prove exceedingly difficult.

He smiled.

Melting it down, it is!

The ground vibrated, and he felt a thumping in his chest. He slowly rose, looking about for the source, when suddenly half a dozen massive helicopters appeared on the horizon, rockets erupting from their weapons pods as 7.62mm rounds belched from their cannons. His men were shredded around him and he dove for cover.

Too late.

He shook from the impact as several rounds tore through his torso, knocking him to the ground as agonizing pain racked his body, and the last thing he saw before blacking out, was the pool of blood growing at his side, and the cheering Americans emerging from the church.

Ganno half crawled, half stumbled, toward the wires for the explosives, the excruciating pain threatening to overwhelm him. The bloody stump where his hand used to be was oozing blood, his belt staunching some of it, but not enough. If he didn't attach the detonator soon, he would pass out, and the Americans would have the Ark.

Helicopters were passing overhead, raining fire down on his country's military, and he felt sorry for them. They were outclassed, outgunned, and stood no chance. They were his countrymen, and their deaths at the hands of the Americans was criminal.

Yet these "innocent" victims had been there for only one reason.

To steal the Ark themselves.

Did it really matter whose hands it fell into? Any hands were too many. The Ark had to be destroyed, and he had only minutes of consciousness left.

He spotted the rock formation hiding the wires and smiled.

Thank you, Lord!

Acton stepped out of the way as the Russians were led up the stairs, reinforcements from two Sea Hawk helicopters mopping up the operation. Dawson entered the room with Red.

"I think it's time we see this thing."

Acton nodded reluctantly. He wasn't certain how he felt about this outcome. Ideally, the Ark would remain with the priests, safely hidden away somewhere, but with the word now out, the search would never end until it was ultimately found.

Safely stored in America is probably best.

He just feared what might happen should someone choose to try and use it.

If it's real.

He just wished he knew for certain.

He led them into the room, shivers rushing over his body at the sight, a sight he could never grow tired of, even if it weren't real. The artisanship, the craftsmanship, that had gone into the creation of the relic, was astonishing. And it *was* a relic. He had no doubt of that, merely from the condition of the wood they had seen.

He simply had no idea if it was *the* relic, or if there ever had been a genuine article.

Dawson whistled in appreciation, shaking his head. He pointed at their newly built chamber. "Is this your handiwork?"

Laura nodded. "Yes. This is why we were brought here."

Dawson took a photo with his phone. "The brass want proof."

Acton motioned toward the phone. "Can you send me that? We weren't allowed to take any photos."

Dawson winked. "Sure, just don't tell anyone." He surveyed the room. "What's the best way to get it out of here?"

Acton shrugged. "Up the stairs, I guess. But we should talk to Father Amanuel first. He'd know best."

"Who's he?"

"He's the Keeper, he's responsible for the Ark."

Dawson waved a hand at the room. "Then where is he?"

Acton's eyes narrowed, spinning on his heel as he looked about. "I don't know. I haven't seen him since the firefight began."

Laura grunted. "Which one?"

Acton shrugged. "The first one, before the Russians. You?"

Laura shook her head. "I haven't seen him either."

Acton scratched his chin. "So, that means he's been gone for what, an hour?"

Laura nodded. "Could be. Time kind of flies when you're being shot at."

Dawson stepped out of the room, barking orders to his men. "Okay, people, let's search the place. We're looking for a priest!"

Niner cursed, Ganno nowhere to be found. He hauled open the door to confirm what he already knew then jumped back. "Holy shit!"

"What?"

Niner pointed at the front seat and Atlas peered through the passenger window. "Are you kidding me? If that doesn't say fanatic, I don't know what does."

Niner agreed, poking the severed hand with the barrel of his MP5.

"What? Are you expecting it to crawl or something?"

Niner shrugged. "Just making sure. I've never actually seen one voluntarily hacked off before." He pointed at the machete. "That had to hurt."

Atlas grunted. "Not sure he'd call it voluntary."

"Well, let's go collect him before he causes any more trouble." They followed the blood trail for a couple hundred feet and found their former prisoner hunched over something. Niner sighed. "You just don't know when to give up, do you, Mr. Ganno?"

Ganno turned, something gripped in his hand, wires leading to a pile of rocks.

Atlas raised his weapon. "What have you got there?"

Ganno held it up and Niner cursed, raising his own weapon as he recognized the crude detonator. "And just what do you plan to do with that?"

"My duty."

"Which is?"

"To destroy the Ark should it be at risk of falling into the wrong hands."

Niner unclipped his MP5, lowering it to the ground, then raising his hands as he approached the rapidly weakening man. "Listen, let's talk about this. Maybe we can figure this out together."

Ganno shook his head. "It's too late. Too many know." He held up the detonator gripped in his one remaining hand. "Don't come any closer. Tell your friends if they want to live, to get out of the church now."

Atlas whispered into his comm behind Niner, relaying the warning.

"Look, let's talk about this. I'm sure we can come to some arrangement."

The man collapsed to his side, his hand shaking. "No, my duty is clear, and my time grows short. Get your friends out. I don't know how much longer I can hold on."

Niner cursed, his eyes bulging. "It's a dead man's switch!"

"BD, get out of there, now! He's got a dead man's switch!"

"Everybody out! Now! This place is gonna blow!"

Acton spun toward Dawson, unsure of what was going on, the Bravo Team already executing their orders without question as everyone rushed toward the stairs. "What about the Ark?"

"Forget it! There's no time!" Dawson grabbed him by the shirt, dragging him toward the stairs. Acton turned, looking for Laura, and reached out for her as she followed them out of the chamber and into the fading sunlight that filtered down from overhead. She rushed up the stairs after the others, Acton following, Dawson taking up the rear.

Suddenly a massive rumble shook the area and Acton pushed as hard as he could up the final steps, then sprinted with the others away from the ancient stone structure. He glanced over his shoulder and gasped as rock, dust, and debris shot out of the earth, chunks of stone of all sizes raining down on them. Laura dropped to the ground, covering her head, and he threw his body over hers as they were peppered with debris.

And then it was over.

An eerie silence fell over the area, punctuated with the occasional sound of a falling rock, but nothing else. The dust began to settle, a gentle breeze clearing away the haze of pulverized rock, and Acton slowly rose to his feet, helping Laura up. They all cautiously approached the hole where the church had been, and Acton gasped.

All that was left inside was a pile of rubble, as if a controlled detonation had been executed flawlessly.

"The Ark!"

It was futile, but he had to know. He rushed forward and picked his way down the steps, still intact, carved into the outer wall and relatively safe from the detonation clearly triggered underneath the church. He climbed over the rubble, toward where the Ark should be, and was startled to find Laura beside him.

She cried out and pointed. Acton collapsed on his haunches at the sight of fragments of their chamber strewn about, along with twisted pieces of gold and shattered wood, nothing left bigger than a fist to suggest what had once been here.

The Sons of Tamrin had succeeded.

The Ark was no more.

The prophecy could be fulfilled.

"What now?"

Acton turned to see Dawson and several of the others behind them. Acton shrugged. "I don't know."

"Does it have any power left?"

"I don't know if it ever did."

"Okay, we'll send a cleanup team in to collect everything we can. Let's get you guys out of here before anyone else shows up."

They climbed the steps in silence, a nearby Sea Hawk powering up.

"What about us?" asked the Russian.

Dawson looked at the prisoners and shook his head. "You're civilians, and this isn't our jurisdiction. You're free to go."

Acton frowned. "I'd give you a stern lecture about stealing ancient relics, but I think it would probably be wasted."

The Russian shrugged. "Probably."

Dawson flicked his wrist at them. "Cut them loose."

Spock and Jimmy drew their knives, cutting the ties binding the surviving Russians. The leader approached, his hand extended. Dawson shook it, then, reluctantly, Acton and Laura.

"Until we meet again."

The Russians walked away, picking up their dead laying on stretchers, and Acton shook his head.

"Why do I think that was probably a mistake?"

Dawson grunted. "Because it was. But there's nothing we can do about it." He headed for one of the Sea Hawks. "Let's get out of here before more Ethiopian regulars arrive. Somebody has to have noticed all these boys arriving."

Acton took one last look at the church, now a pile of rubble. "I can't believe it's gone."

Laura gripped his hand. "I know."

Her voice cracked, and he tore his eyes away from what once was. "Hey, what's with the tears? I thought you didn't believe in it?"

She shook her head. "I never said that, I just said I wasn't sure. What if it was real? And now it's gone, all because we tried to preserve it."

Acton put an arm over her shoulder and held her close. "No, because Father Amanuel tried to preserve it. This isn't our fault."

She sighed. "I guess not, though I do feel somewhat responsible."

Acton paused, spinning back toward the church. "Speaking of Father Amanuel, where do you think he went?"

Laura turned and they both peered into the hole. "Hopefully he escaped somehow. He didn't deserve to die."

Acton frowned, spotting a piece of what was once an intricately sculpted cherub. "No, but he may wish he had."

Acton Residence

St. Paul, Maryland

Acton winced as Laura stepped into the bedroom, toweling dry after a long soak in the bathtub. She was covered in bruises and scrapes, and he blamed himself. "I think you got the worst of it this time."

She rotated her shoulders gingerly. "Lucky me." She dropped the towel on the floor then flopped on the bed, her legs spread, her arms outstretched. "Flip me over so I can dry the front."

Acton chuckled. "I'm dressed, what if I just got on top of—"

"Don't you even think about it!"

He grinned then picked up her towel, gently drying her off. "I think you'll be calling in sick for a few days."

"I think my boss will want to know why."

"Tell him the truth."

"What, that my husband shoved me down a set of stone stairs carved into the bedrock in Ethiopia because Russian art thieves were shooting at us while they tried to steal the Ark of the Covenant?"

"Exactly!"

She eyed him. "He might just believe me. Who could make something like that up?"

His phone vibrated on the nightstand and he leaned over to grab it. It was a text message from a number he didn't recognize. He swiped his thumb and gasped at the photo attached. "Well, if you need proof..." He handed the phone to Laura with the photo of the Ark, obviously sent by Dawson.

She stared at it, sighing. "It's so sad. Something so precious lost because of greed." She squinted and gripped the phone in both hands, using her thumbs to zoom in on the photo.

Then gasped, her eyes shooting wide. "Oh my God!"

Acton tensed. "What?"

"Look!" She handed the phone back to him and Acton stared at the zoomed in image, not sure what his wife was excited about.

Then he saw it.

And nearly fainted.

"The poles! They're intact!"

Laura sat upright, her pain forgotten, as they both stared at the photo. "The real Ark had a broken one!"

A smile spread across Acton's face. "That clever bastard! He switched it while we were fighting over it. There must have been a secret passage. He probably already had a fake in place, just in case anyone followed us."

A tear rolled down Laura's cheek as she leaned against him, resting her head on his shoulder. "So, it's still out there, somewhere. It's a miracle he was able to switch everything in time."

Acton smiled, squeezing her tight. "And God doesn't waste those on fake artifacts."

THE END

ACKNOWLEDGMENTS

While writing this novel, a great tragedy happened. A good friend of mine, Glen Goudie, passed away, apparently from two aneurysms and a stroke. He was only in his early fifties. Glen and I worked together for years as IT consultants on government contracts, both of us Project Leaders on sister projects at one point. We became friends, and after I left, maintained casual contact including the occasional lunch.

A few weeks before this writing, I had thought I should call him to do lunch. It had been years, and becoming lost in the solitary life of a writer is a trap too easily fallen into. I was too busy at the time, and in a lot of pain, so said the typical thing one says in these cases: I'll call him later.

I rarely use Facebook beyond communicating with my readers. I find it a major time-suck, filled with drivel. Yes, there are lots of funny things there, and interesting things about friends and family, but I just don't have the time for that. A couple of weeks ago, I did have some spare time one evening, and clicked that little F.

And found out my friend had died the night before.

It hit me a little harder than I had expected, since I hadn't seen him in so long. I think it was because we were similar in age, had similar careers until I became a writer, and he even started dating a Filipina after his divorce. It made me think that his fate could be mine. It also made me think about how we so often think there's plenty of time left to do something, to see someone, to try some new thing.

And then suddenly, in the blink of an eye, there isn't.

Dying with regrets I think is unavoidable, but when one of those regrets could have been avoided by just picking up a phone, or blocking off an hour for lunch, that is sad. There might be reasons. In my situation, I've had many health issues over the past decade that have caused me to lose touch with a lot of my friends, and what makes it worse, is that many have no idea why.

When I reached out to some friends to find out exactly what had happened to Glen, I discovered email addresses no longer worked, and realized just how out of touch I was. Thankfully, one still did, and he responded with what I needed to know, and warmed my heart by suggesting he and another friend from my past come and visit me at my home, since I couldn't come to them.

It's easy to forget how isolated some people can become through no fault of their own. So, if you have an old friend or family member you haven't heard from in a while, perhaps there's a reason, and a simple phone call, email, or visit, might brighten their day.

I know it always brightens mine.

As usual, there are people to thank. My dad for all the research, Ian Kennedy for some explosives info, Brent Richards for some weapons info, and, as usual, my wife, daughter, and mother, as well as the proofing and launch teams.

To those who have not already done so, please visit my website at www.jrobertkennedy.com then sign up for the Insider's Club to be notified of new book releases. Your email address will never be shared or sold, and you'll only receive the occasional email from me, as I don't have time to spam you!

Thank you once again for reading.

Made in the USA
Las Vegas, NV
30 June 2023